W9-CIG-685

American Meteor

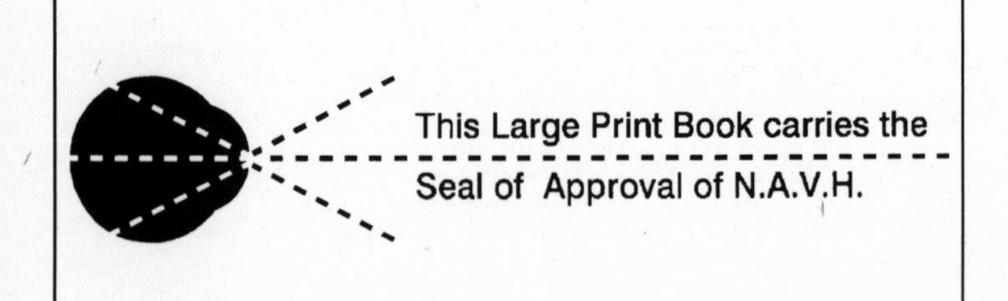
This Large Print Book carries the
Seal of Approval of N.A.V.H.

American Meteor

Norman Lock

THORNDIKE PRESS
A part of Gale, Cengage Learning

GALE
CENGAGE Learning

Farmington Hills, Mich • San Francisco • New York • Waterville, Maine
Meriden, Conn • Mason, Ohio • Chicago

Copyright © 2015 by Norman Lock.
Thorndike Press, a part of Gale, Cengage Learning.

ALL RIGHTS RESERVED

This is a work of fiction. Characters, organizations, events, and places (even those that are actual) are either products of the author's imagination or are used fictitiously.

Thorndike Press® Large Print Western.
The text of this Large Print edition is unabridged.
Other aspects of the book may vary from the original edition.
Set in 16 pt. Plantin.

LIBRARY OF CONGRESS CATALOGING-IN-PUBLICATION DATA

Lock, Norman, 1950–
American meteor / Norman Lock. — Large print edition.
pages cm. — (Thorndike Press large print western)
ISBN 978-1-4104-8214-3 (hardback) — ISBN 1-4104-8214-6 (hardcover)
1. Large type books. I. Title.
PS3562.O218A84 2015b
813'.54—dc23 2015025057

Published in 2015 by arrangement with Bellevue Literary Press

Printed in Mexico
1 2 3 4 5 6 7 19 18 17 16 15

For Helen

What am I myself
but one of your meteors?

— Walt Whitman,
"Year of Meteors"

Part One: Lincoln

This then is life . . .

— Walt Whitman,
Starting from Paumanok

Armory Square Hospital, Washington City,
April 13, 1865

I got so I could disentangle from the general stink the various odors that combined in an evil and rancid atmosphere, oppressing the sound, the maimed, and the dying alike. My nose, always a perceptive organ, would search among the currents of stagnating air, like a monkey's snuffling delicately over a tempting morsel (filth, to you and me). I soon learned to recognize the different fumes of carbolic, pine tar, iodine, cigar smoke, whiskey, turpentine, creosote, blood, gore, lamp oil, sweat, paraffin, and the reeking contents of bedpans noisy with the riot of flies. I lay on the cot in a drowse, moving only to swat at them — sight halved by a bandage over my eye.

Bored, I would watch the bloodstained surgeons and nurses passing to and fro, in frantic haste or in weariness, among long rows of cots that would seem, in their regularity, like cemetery plots if it weren't for the thrashing of bodies consigned to their untidy sheets. My good eye fixed on the rafters overhead, I would not have known that the man next to me, whose blasted leg had been hauled away in a slop bucket, was still among the living if it hadn't been for his infernal groans. I swear I'm not ashamed to say that, on more than one occasion, I wished him dead. I couldn't sleep, you see, because of the ache in my socket after its eye had been put out by a red-hot piece of rebel shell.

Lowering my gaze (if a one-eyed boy could be said to have a gaze) from the high ceiling, gauzy and sallow now with the smoke of the surgeons' stogies, the ill-trimmed lamps, and coal stoves topped by madly rattling tubs where women, forearms beefy as any man's, stirred boiling water in which sheets and dressings stewed, I looked at the pair of boots, forlorn beneath my neighbor's cot. Henceforth, he would require only one of them.

Although I'd been sick before and once,

with scarlet fever, at death's door, I'd never been inside a hospital until now. It was only natural for me to take an interest in the grim proceedings: I was sixteen and curious, like any other boy. Maybe if I'd been gravely wounded, I'd have been less able to view my surroundings dispassionately. But what pain I had was dulled by laudanum. All in all, I felt like a god must who comes, incognito, among his creatures — one of lowly rank and stature, but a divinity nonetheless, who can tranquilly survey the wreckage of his creation.

Meditating — war had made me thoughtful — on the diverse ways a person may be recast by bullet, fire, or gangrene, I didn't hear the man in an open-collared shirt and slouch hat bend over the ruined soldier next to me; didn't hear him utter words of comfort while he dressed the weeping wound. So lost in my own hellish thoughts, I started and nearly cried out in surprise when he put his hand softly on my shoulder and, with his other, brushed the hair from my eye (the one that used to be). I'd have cursed him for his familiarity and interference — we were often interfered with by Bible-beaters, their damned turnip faces tearful or cunning in the lust for our souls — but something in this man's face — its frank look and sad, almost puzzled smile — and in the gentleness of his hand as it lay so cool and nice on my feverish cheek made me hold my tongue.

Besides, I'd seen him before.

Brooklyn and Manhattan, 1860–1861

Barelegged and shoeless, I stood against the sea — the salty remnant that swept into Sheepshead Bay — casting broken shells on the beach the Indians called "Land Without Shadows." I considered myself a remarkable boy who, with the strength of Hercules, broke at every step the iron shackles meant, by a stern ocean, to hobble him. I was twelve — or nearly — on that September evening, with the whole of Brooklyn at my back and, beyond it, Staten Island and, in the unimaginable distance, the West unrolling like an enormous wave of soil, granite, and trees clear to the Pacific, which was said to be blue and reefed with coral. They took oysters there, also — oysters like ours, big as dinner plates, to sell on the Barbary Coast, just as I sold what I managed to rake up from the shallows to saloons and eateries from Coenties Slip to Gouverneur Lane. My stooped back aching with the work and with the sodden canvas bag, heavy with oyster shells, hung across it, I stood up in time to see a fat gull's transit from air to water, legs crumpling under wings frantic to find again their gracefulness. It was a clumsy moment, saved by the low sun that gilded bird and wave alike. I noticed, out the corner of my eye (I had two of them then), the man who'd later kneel beside my cot in the Washington City hospital at the very end of Mr. Lincoln's War. The "wound dresser" bore slight resemblance to this person capering on the wet sand, as if each of the four intervening years of war had tolled twice for him in sorrow, so aged and harrowed did he seem. But in 1860, he looked to be the youthful and vigorous man he was, although he behaved like a lunatic crazed by the seething tide. Those were nervous times. From "Bleeding Kansas" to Harper's Ferry, the contagion had been spreading like fire through the rooms of a house, and only the senile or the insane, whose nerves hummed to quite different vibrations, might escape the universal jangle.

He was muttering some prayer — or so it seemed to me, a boy who'd stood oftentimes on a Sunday morning outside the Methodist church to hear the hymns. The man stood, hat in hand, as if in the presence of the Almighty or a Gravesend copper — his throat moving impolitely, as might that of a man who'd swallowed raw whiskey. He was a sight! Abruptly, the wind picked up, as it will in September before nightfall, and gusts of words — strange and thrilling — came within my hearing, mixed with the noise of water dragging over gravel and broken shells: "You oceans that have been calm within me! how I feel you, fathomless, stirring, preparing unprecedented waves and storms." Those were brave-sounding words to a boy hankering for adventure, with the salt burning his lips — a boy not knowing before this moment that he wished to throw off the yoke of his miserable days. I nearly threw off the oyster bag, but I didn't, fearing my father's razor strop.

The wind fell away and, with it, the words of the lunatic, which no longer reached me. Surely, he must be one, the way he stood there, with the rising water picking at his boot laces — oblivious and mouthing blessings or obscenities at the trembling horizon! The exultation left me, like water squeezed from a sponge, and my heart grew sad. Perhaps it was the flooding tide, which made in the dusky light the same sad music were a band to play a heartrending adagio.

I turned and, pulling the streaming bag after me, left the ocean, the beach, and, for all I knew, the world to its last darkness. I hurried across Coney Island Creek toward the Hope & Anchor to sell my sweet harvest.

After that night, which I've never ceased to think of as marvelous (forty-some years later, I cannot recall it without a thrilling sensation at the back of my neck), I seemed to see the man everywhere I went: leaning, nonchalant, against the taffrail on the Brooklyn ferry, jawing with the teamster on a Broadway streetcar, loafing with roughnecks by Gowanus Creek, cooing over bedraggled pigeons in Battery Park, and flushed and rowdy in taprooms up and down Pearl, Fulton, and Water streets. Always, the man seemed to wind himself outlandishly among his fellows, as if to entangle himself en masse in them — an arm thrown congenially around their necks, embracing them all, bestowing a brotherly kiss on the bearded lips of them all. A wicker hamper of oysters at my feet, I'd watch with amazement while he sauntered amid a crowd of men and women who seemed not the least put out by his wildness. He was, I thought, a one-man circus or a freak show whose candor couldn't embarrass me — not after having spent my childhood in a tenement house, with only a curtain dividing our half of the room from our neighbors'. Early on, I knew the ways of men and women and how they would grapple in love, misery, and in hatred, sometimes with a ferocity that drove me out onto the streets, where the night — its tonic, unpent air and its calm stars — silenced the clamor of my heart.

In November 1861, I joined the "13th Brooklyn," as the 87th New York Regiment was called, and went to war. My last look at Brooklyn — though not at Walt Whitman, as I would come to know my lunatic — was at the ferry slip where the regiment embarked on the steamboat *Marion* for Washington City, after a send-off at Fort Greene. His Honor, the mayor of Brooklyn, had declared in an aria of high-flown flapdoodle that the "flag will have to be born aloft through seas of blood," including, as it turned out, mine. I would never again see the city of my birth and rearing, but Whitman — him I'd see in the Armory Square Hospital and, years later, in Camden. We didn't speak or even so much as acknowledge each other on the ferry dock. He didn't recognize the oyster boy who had unwittingly overheard his thoughts on the coming storm, in which I was now about to be engulfed and, later, would be struck down.

Whitman moved amid the crowd of

hoarse-throated soldiers, setting down the departing words of some in a notebook until he was swallowed up by fluttering handkerchiefs, brandished stovepipe hats, and particles of soot that descended from the *Marion*'s funnels in memory of our departure. Later, I would learn that the man I seemed all year to have dogged through the streets of lower Manhattan had recently been the editor of the *Brooklyn Daily Times.* He accompanied us during the last few hours of our youthfulness — suffering with us the fulminations of a righteous gang of government stooges and starched churchmen; parading with us down Myrtle Avenue into Prince Street, into Gold, and on to Vinegar Hill and the ferry depot to stand with us on the pier above the East River, where we waited impatiently to throw ourselves into the pit that hath no bottom. For so it proved to be. He did not take down *my* words, and I would have had none to give him.

I stood at the rail of the *Marion,* next to William Kidd, the regimental drummer who'd lose at Groveton something more vital to breath than an eye; and I bugled a martial air to silence the patriotic mob so that Marie Bisbee, of Brooklyn, could shout her farewell poem at us. She went at it hammer and tongs. Lucky for you, Jay, I remember just the first words:

It is the martial sound of drum,
The thrilling pipe is heard!
And now alas! the hour has come,
To say the parting word.
Farewell brave youths, to battle field
Thy country calls thee now!
May He who does the widow shield,
Watch o'er thy fervid brow.

We weren't taken in by her horseshit — at least Little Will and I weren't. He looked at me slyly, two fingers pinching his nostrils shut in disgust, while I blew the spit out of my horn.

Aboard the Steamer Marion, December 1861

In recollection, all our bivouacs and battlefields were alike, at least for those of us who did their living and fighting and oftentimes their dying there. War's architects saw them from loftier vantages where, in Union blue or Confederate gray, soldiers were no more than meteors or moths, uniform, fugitive, and doomed. Soon enough, I grew to hate warfare and took no interest in its bewildering strategies or reckless campaigns, as monotonous as the tunes

I blew on my bugle, which I had named Jericho in honor of Joshua's trumpet.

When I first arrived in Lincoln — in 1882, that was, before you came out here — I played the trumpet in the town's brass band. I wasn't much good, and the burden of sociability proved too much for me to stay with it. But I was one hell of a bugle boy, Jay, and I wish you could've heard me!

The bugle — one day I'll have its likeness carved on my headstone — tells a story of its own concerning my service with the 13th — days neither thrilling nor glorious: a dent gotten at Bull Run during the Great Skedaddle, our panicked troops snarled in the rout of picnickers who'd driven out from the capital to enjoy a festive day of slaughter; another dent gotten at Yorktown, when I was nearly trampled by a horse; another, at Oak Grove, compliments of a Johnny Reb sharpshooter who must have thought my tunes sour; and still another at Chantilly, where our regimental strength was so bled that the enlisted men among us were incorporated into the 173rd New York Infantry. The 87th Regiment having been disbanded, our officers went home to swagger in their uniforms.

A slightly built thirteen-year-old recruit, I was too weak to handle a musket. By the time I'd grown into one, I was too practiced a bugler to swap it for a firearm. The adjutants often complimented me on the clarity of my renditions of "Assembly," "Call to Quarters," "Boots and Saddles," "Go Forward," "To the Left," "To the Right," "About," "Rally on the Chief," "Trot," "Gallop," "Rise Up," "Lay Down," "Commence Firing," "Cease Firing," "Disperse," and that ever-popular air among soldiers, "Retreat." Those of the opinion that the worst a bugler had to fear was an angry boot shied at him for crowing reveille at dawn are mistaken. It required an imperturbable disposition to stand and tootle, in a commotion of men and horses, in a confusion of smoke so thick and acrid that it would blind us with tears and choke us with the bitterness of war. But this is not a story about war — not even so grisly and scarifying a one as our own Civil War. Suffice it to say that, during four years of terror and mayhem, I bugled my way, like a worm traversing a dog's guts, through historic battles (notable for their casualties), whose hallowed grounds one day would be picturesque destinations for tourists armed with Kodaks and charged with the discipline of ice-cream-eating brats. Bull Run, Yorktown, Williamsburg, Seven Pines, Oak

Grove, Malvern Hill, Harrison's Landing, Groveton, Second Bull Run, Chantilly — those "curious panics" that became a national obsession and our common property, whether we'd fought in them or not.

We would stall outside Richmond, and — blow as heroically as I might — I could not persuade General McClellan out of his damned timidity to advance, although Jericho surely put the fear of God into many a Jeff Davis boy, who, like me, were frightened out of their wits. If I'd been armed with something that expended lead rather than breath, I'd have shot our half-pint general gladly. I've killed only three men during my fifty-three years aboveground in our beautiful, spacious, and altogether murderous country. I can't say whether or not they deserved their fates, though I had good reason at the time to pack them off to glory or perdition.

Because the skirmishes and slaughters in which I played a part, however small, appear in my mind to have been all of a piece, I'll relate the battle in which I gave up my eye for the Union and the slaves — and let it stand for them all. To be truthful, I was in no almighty hurry to benefit the latter, never having known a black man to speak to until, much later, I fell into the Delaware and was fished out by one.

But before I recount the Battle of Five Forks, Virginia, I want to say something about our boat trip from Brooklyn to Washington City. You'd have thought we were on a weekend excursion, the way we carried on. On deck, the regimental band (its members would be sent home to mothers and sweethearts after the rough going on the Peninsula) played "America the Beautiful," "The Star-Spangled Banner," "John Brown's Body," and a number of sweet airs like Stephen Foster's "The Village Maiden" and "Beautiful Dreamer." The bugle was considered uncouth, and bugle boys were shunned by the band's high-toned personnel, outlandishly dressed like French soldiers in North Africa: Zouave jackets, red pants, white leggings, blue sashes tied around their waists — the insanity topped off by white turbans!

While the men swallowed the treacle served up above, Little Will and I sweat over craps with the stokers in the infernal weather of the steamboat's hold. *Craps* — a vulgar word whose origin is *crapaud,* meaning "toad" in French — refers to a crap shooter's squat, if you're curious. We must paper ourselves with facts, even if we are mistaken in them. I would not tell you to lie, although it would not behoove you to be overly fastidious concerning the truth. Conjecture and speculation are how the West was won, and much else besides. In any case, craps suited us fine, and I would have lost my bugle to a coal-blackened son of a bitch if a sergeant hadn't smelled us out and kicked Little Will and me topside with his brand-new boots. They'd look like hell's own pitch after we landed in Washington City, where the December mud swallowed horses and caissons whole.

All along the East River and through the Narrows, people stood and cheered, waving hats and babies in the air and shouting after us to "hang Jeff Davis from a sour apple tree." There is no gaiety to equal that hatched by rancor. Fire company bands blared fighting tunes, and a skiff overloaded with drunks tried to foist a trio of barroom floozies on us. We cheered *that,* I can tell you! But the sailors, swearing under their breath at the intolerance of authority, were ordered to drive them off with poles.

"It's a shame to throw a fat fish back into the water," Little Will said.

I took his meaning, but I supposed we were too green to have gotten much by way of nourishment from a floozy, even if we had been afforded the opportunity.

"I've got a firecracker in my pocket," I said to prove I was a hell-raiser, too.

"Let's toss it down the Charlie Noble," he replied, referring to the copper stack venting the galley.

I lit the cracker and dropped it down the stack. To the discerning ears of two hellions, it produced a most agreeable sound, like a pig's bladder when pent-up air is suddenly let loose. The squib set pots and pans to chiming and roused the cook from his greasy lair, armed with a knife useful in flaying carcasses. Only the boat's yawing saved us from a terrible end. Little Will and I crawled into a lifeboat and fell asleep while Barbados rum was ladled into tins to revive the courage of men whose hearts, like bobbins, were being emptied with each nautical mile of the mystic thread of affection — their heart's needle listing to the north. By the time the war was finished, the thread would stretch almost to breaking. On that night aboard the *Marion,* many knew an ecstasy they would not know again, except for a few of them who would find a transporting madness in murder. Those, I think, were the truly damned among us — lives blasted away from the common thoroughfare.

Unseen by Little Will and me, who were kept a while longer blameless and unharmed in childish sleep, the *Marion* steamed along the Brooklyn and Long Island coasts and then into the Atlantic. Black smoke pouring from her stacks, she hurried southward — rounding the Delaware peninsula, past Fort Monroe — and entered Chesapeake Bay and on to the Potomac River. Often, during the four years to come, she'd steam north through the Narrows to Vinegar Hill — a likely Calvary — her hold packed with Union soldiers wearing wooden coats. In the days after the Draft Riots, the northbound *Marion* might have passed corpses of former slaves lynched and butchered by New York's resentful poor — their bodies dumped into the East River and left for the currents to carry them, resignedly, south into everlasting captivity.

Washington City, December 1861–March 1862

What boy wouldn't be satisfied with days spent playing soldier? That's what it was like to be in the Army of the Potomac that first winter in Washington City, when the only hardships were mud, which was of a sovereign quality, in keeping with our nation's capital; rats that deserted the riverbank to join the Union's sprawl of tents (the rats, too, were sovereign); and the wringer of the interminable drills McClellan put us through while he sat on his high horse, with a hand — like Bonaparte's — tucked up inside his coat. We were lucky to have missed the Washingtonian mosquito, said to be reared in the pestilential swamps to possess a sparrow's heft and the sting of a cottonmouth.

On second thought, our bivouac on the Potomac grew stale. Even so engrossing a bit of theater as pretending to kill rebel soldiers with musket or bayonet can become tedious. I missed Broadway and the Battery, the Brooklyn saloons where I sold oysters and, too often, coaxed and kicked my old man home (if you could call it that) from his stupefying and inglorious binges. How fondly I remembered hearing in an Ocean Avenue barroom a waltz tune, cheerful among the shiftless — notes falling unheeded, like gobs of spittle on the sawdust-sprinkled floor! I missed Sheepshead Bay and would gladly have stood up to my knees in winter salt water, raking oysters till my arms dropped off, to be back there again.

I became an expert on my instrument, as Little Will did on his drum. We also became veterans of the boudoir, although the girl on whom we practiced lay not in a swank bedroom on tasseled pillows, but in a hut where black-bound testaments and chaplains' issues of holy gear were stored. We were too young, Little Will and I, to savor the delicious incongruity. I mean, goddamn it, we gave no thought to irony and none at all to love while we strained after the satisfaction said to fill a man lying in a woman's lap. To me, it felt like riding a lumpy sack of meal. We were also too young to realize that what a woman is willing to sell a man will not slake, for long, the passion in which he boils.

"Did you enjoy yourself any?" I asked Little Will afterward, while we ran combs through our tousled hair.

"I'd rather wrestle an alligator," he said, and I had to agree.

Having no more to say on the subject, we ran off to play baseball with other soldiers of Company B who were, like us, temporarily at loose ends. We would look back on this time of childish folly and insouciance with fierce longing, as old men will on the perished days of their youth. Soon enough, we'd all be hotfooting it in hell's vestibule. But we'd have some colorful tales to tell — those of us who didn't get themselves scorched.

One day, when I will keep the long hours of eternity below my island of grass, I expect to trade stories with dead folk of every kind, color, and previous occupation. In the cemetery, all men and women are contemporaries; all, the comrades and intimates Walt Whitman praised in his *Leaves,* with a foolish optimism born of an infatuated heart (you can die of such a heart!) — foolish, because only after we've passed into glory or oblivion is the perfect comradeship and intimacy he espoused possible. I've often thought how splendid it would be if I could talk to Whitman now. I'd ask him if it is really just as lucky to die as it is to be born. But there is a continent flung between us, whose great divide is more obdurate than granite. One day, when day is meaningless and indistinguishable from night, I hope to find answers to the questions that have vexed me — unless oblivion does win out over the Rapture and eternity is as silent as the tomb.

One question concerns me, myself: Why did I often find it necessary to lie?

Take the story of how I came to lose my eye. Between you and me, it wasn't the fault of a Confederate shell, as I like to let on, but of my ignorance and panic during the charge at Five Forks. A Union rifleman beside me dropped, with a minié ball through his heart. The Johnny Reb who'd fired it stood ten feet away, preparing to do the same to me, regardless of my tender years and noncombatant status as a bugle boy. I picked up the dead man's Enfield, poured black powder down its throat, chased it with a lead ball, and then — hands shaking — rammed ball and powder home. Next, I set the percussion cap, cocked the hammer, and fired. I made a mess of it, however, and the spark burned my eye. When it became infected, an army surgeon spooned it out. But I'll tell you this: My manhood hinged on the idea — call it a "fact" — that a rebel howitzer put out my eye. Much of what followed and added up to my life had its origin in the tale I told later on to Whitman. Anyway, it makes a better story — the way I always told it. Don't you think?

The rebel I had meant to shoot stepped toward me over gray stubble and dead men of both factions, intending to brain me with the butt end of his musket. I still recall how his eyes — they did not shine — looked dead and goggled, like those of a fish at its last gasp. I think he resented me because he was obliged to kill me. I reached toward him with my bayonet, idly, as you might fork up a last morsel of meat, though your appetite was lost; touched the place where his vital spirits congregated; and watched him dangle a moment (long as eternity) and then drop. I had killed my first man. I wonder if I meant to. No, I don't think will or even wish entered into it. I pierced him as mindlessly as a dead frog will jerk when given a galvanic shock. It was a case of murder by accident.

Five Forks, Virginia, April 1, 1865

I'll describe, as well as I am able, the Battle of Five Forks and then be done with the war, except for its aftermath. I say "as well as I am able" not to make a show of modesty but, rather, to acknowledge the befuddled senses of a man in battle, where fear, misery, noise, cannon and musket smoke make for each combatant a kind of bell jar. Think of an insect trapped under glass. What must it feel — if so lowly a creature can be said to feel — to find itself all of a sudden cut off from the world it knew? That's what it's like for a man in a fight for his life. To be separated profoundly from his intellect; to exist solely in his body; to be preoccupied entirely with the body's survival. To hell with the mind! Inside the bell jar, a man has no more to do with thoughts, doctrines, a cause célèbre, his previous sentiments and affections than a bug would. Life, its color and complexity, is reduced — like a mess of stew bones boiling in a pot — to an elemental dish whose simple flavors are rue and terror, hatred and self-love.

There are heroes — I would not tell you otherwise. But the dish they eat at what might be the hour of their death is the same. Willingly or reluctantly, we went to be tried; eagerly or tearfully, we marched for union or abolition. But the moment when we stood on the scaffold raised over the abyss, we were deaf to Lincoln's proclamations and the orders of the generals — hearing only the bestial noise of the shambles or what sound a gigantic maw might make opening wide to receive us. There is no reliable witness to a slaughter, just as none die happily or well who die in war.

I remember smoke — how it lazed above us, like a low-lying cloud or like the bluish gray mist fraying above wan fields after the morning sun has burned off the dew. In the old woods bordering the field, ruts clogged with April mud, torn bandages of smoke clung to the bones of the leafless chestnut trees (a species soon to be no more). The gloomy aisles were treacherous with thickets and downed branches turned gray, like the deer and squirrels, by winter. Dropped leaves left to rot above the thankful grubs were slick with recent rain. Knowing no way to say how war is, the qualities that make it a thing wholly unto itself, I must resort to a literary language that denatures it. What birds and animals claimed Five Forks as their habitat had fled, panicked by the hobnailed armies of Sheridan and Pickett, met in those dun woods and fields — the one to strike the vital Southside Railroad, the other to defend it at all cost for Lee and the Confederacy.

That afternoon, we threaded our way through underbrush that tangled us in thorns and whipcords, as if the vegetation sided with the Army of Northern Virginia against us Yankees. Out of the woods at last, we charged the entrenchments set along White Oak Road, only to find the enemy's center had moved during our painstaking march through the trees. We shambled in confusion until Warren flung us recklessly against the rebel line — this time from the north — while Sheridan swept Pickett's left with his cavalry, destroying it. You may have seen the famous lithograph.

As a result of that April day in the year 1865 (I will not call it the Lord's), Pickett lost a third of his army, Lee lost Petersburg,

Jeff Davis lost Richmond, the Confederacy lost the war, and I lost my eye. Before that day, I had not thought blood could be so red! It lay in crimson drops on the palms of dead leaves, like that from Christ's own wounds; it dripped garnets from the briar thorns; it turned to scarlet the sodden furrows cut in peaceable days by plowshares (abandoned, since, to rust — blood's other color), as if Aaron had walked among them with his vengeful rod. I tell you the fields were soaked, the stubble blazed with it! I'd never seen what a garish thing blood is until my eye socket brimmed with it! The Battle of Five Forks halved my sight and did as much as any of that uncivil war's campaigns to stitch up the Union.

This blab of mine isn't meant to be a history of the Civil War and what followed it: I mean the wrong turnings made in realizing a destiny consecrated by deception, fraud, murder, and profit. No, I wish only to study the sickness of the degenerate age in which I lie at night, listening to the boasts and grievances of the dead: a faculty forged by blinding headaches that beset me after the death of Crazy Horse. Your headache powders would've been useless against them, Jay, and you'd have had to look elsewhere for their cause than a clinch knot in the brain. I doubt your arts take in the supernatural. No, you're a hardheaded Yankee doc and can't credit what your science won't allow — but indulge me awhile. What I have to say makes for one hell of a yarn, if nothing else.

Armory Square Hospital, Washington City, April 13–21, 1865

I could not have known that the train that carried me from Five Forks to the army surgeons in Washington — the first I'd ever ridden — would herald, with a noise of tortured iron and escaping steam, a future delivered up to the railroads. I was too enthralled by the novelties of speed, felt by my muscles and nerves as a reluctance, and motion, seen by my unbandaged eye as a blur of woods and fields, rivers and marshland, to think what this journey might portend. Besides, I was not then gifted with foresight, as I'll seem to you to be later on when I recount my days in light of time to come. Wreathed funereally by coal smoke, the train arrived in Washington at the Baltimore & Ohio Depot, where, four years earlier, his life threatened by secessionists, Lincoln had slunk, incognito, into the capital to take his oath. From that same station of his cross, he would leave on a funeral train after having departed this life for the next on Saturday, the fifteenth of April.

On Thursday, I was driven to the Armory Square Hospital and liberally dosed with rye whiskey before my eye socket was cleaned, cauterized, and bandaged. I'd already concocted the story of my heroic charge against a rebel battery, armed with nothing but a B-flat bugle. (Sadly, no lithograph was made, commemorating my musicality and derring-do.) That afternoon, Walt Whitman sidled up to me where I lay on a cot among the wounded, watching cigar smoke write in Persian letters prophesies of my coming life as a man.

Looming like the moon in a fog of mosquito netting, Whitman's face got in the way of my destiny, which, in any case, I couldn't decipher. His countenance was intelligent, kind, but underlain by a fierceness that would blaze up into his tired eyes. Five years earlier, when I'd watched him shout his verses into the evening breeze, his hair, beard, and mustache had been unfashionably neat for that manly age of facial barbarism. They were indifferently kept now, as if pain and sorrow had made the least act of self-regard frivolous to his mind. At Sheepshead Bay, he had resembled the picture of Jesus in the testament later given me by the Christian Sanitary Commission. Now, he appeared as Moses must have after hearing the Almighty speak from the burning bush. His eyes bore into a man, as though he meant to assay the ore of his character. I'd have shivered had his look not also conveyed so large a store of pity. Wrath for what the war had taken was mostly dampened by the better angels of his nature.

I've heard the talk concerning Whitman's depravity, but I never believed it. When he laid his hand gently on my brow, I felt the tenderness of a benevolent man, nothing else. If I had been well and he'd thrown his arm over my shoulder and embraced me — even if he'd kissed me with his bearded lips and called me his sweet comrade — I would not have been ashamed. In my childhood, I had grown beyond shame, and nothing could embarrass me. I'd walked the squalid streets and alleys of the Five Points and the Bowery; passed — an unnoticed boy — among filthy dens where whores, thieves, and cutthroats consorted. I'd seen most every variety of human and bestial conjugation and suffered the hardships of our kind's most ingenious war. There will be others, even more ingenious and brutal. I mean to say that I was not naïve, nor was I the least afraid of this man whose love for men and women seemed perfect Christian zeal.

I knew no other faith; knew of Christ and the mother of God, of His saints and angels only what my Irish mother had taught me before typhoid took her to Abraham's bosom or only to the sure and certain corruption of the body, packed with little ceremony in the impoverished earth of Ward's Island, on the other side of Little Hell Gate. I don't believe in hell, except as it was spread daily before my eyes from Canal Street to Pearl, squeezed into Manhattan's rancid tit between the East River and the Hudson. Hell is for the living. And heaven? A boy, I pictured it as a field of fireflies on a summer's night — each tiny yellow light a blessed soul. If my childish fancy is true, then the end of days for hosanna-hymning bugs lies in the bloated belly of a bat.

"Poor boy," Whitman murmured, as if he had looked into my mind with his all-seeing eyes and found there the common tragedy of the poor.

Grateful for his sympathy, which I knew to be genuine, I nodded my thanks. Like love, it was a delicacy rarely served in tenements where creatures (call them people for old time's sake) swarmed like ants on a stale cake, in spaces (I will not call them rooms) with a dearth of light and air but a plenitude of misery and disease. I had a brother, Sean. Too young for war, he stayed behind in Bushwick with our useless souse of a father. After I left, he went bad (a word used also for spoiled meat beloved by maggots), preferring a roughneck life to the oyster trade. Small and wiry, he excelled as a pick-pocket until a porter found his hand inside his dungarees and broke it. Versatile, he took to waylaying swanks on Wall Street and looting Fifth Avenue kitchens of silverware and plate. Sean moved into the "Bloody Sixth" near the seaport so that he could rob the Irish just off the boat "to give them a taste of equality." When my uncle Jack broke his neck, falling from a streetcar, I had no further news of Sean or of my father. Uncle Jack had beautiful penmanship — strange in a man with fists like beef hearts — and he liked to write letters. Once he'd gone, I would get no others, though envelopes would pass through my hands — links in a chain holding the continent together — while I sorted mail, in motion between Santa Fe and Independence, Missouri.

Ten years ago — it must have been — I was leafing through a book of pictures taken by Jacob Riis, when my hand was stayed by a photograph of "Bandit's Roost" in New York City. In the foreground, my brother stands with swaggering nonchalance, a hand in the pocket of his dark suit. From the shadow of a derby hat, his eyes confront the camera with cold and insolent certainty. His mouth is cruel. Behind him, another man appears to be leaning on the barrel of a rifle, unless it's only a length of steel with which to batter down doors or break heads. In the wet, somber recesses of the alley, between two Mulberry Street tenement houses, overhung with ragged, dingy wash, other roughneck men stare down the interloper, while, from out a window, a sharp-faced woman glares. I wondered then if Sean had died since his picture'd been taken and — for a moment — I hoped he had.

"Were they able to save your eye?" Whitman asked, his voice so drenched in melancholy that my unbandaged orb began to weep in pity for its lost twin.

"No, sir," I said, touching the ravaged place.

He shook his head ruefully and gave me a look that would have softened Herod's flinty heart. When I'd wished my brother dead, I was indulging in the self-righteousness of someone who had already grown away from temptation after capacity and appetite had dulled. I'd never been vicious like Sean, but I had sinned in the usual ways of men and women who did not settle and who lived on the frontiers of existence, under conditions most would consider savage. The ill will I felt toward my brother when I saw him at Bandit's Roost (a fabulous place despite its meanness) might have been envy for a young man still in the prime of life. That he, too, must have aged since Riis had captured him with his box camera didn't occur to me. That day in the Lincoln public library when I saw Sean's picture, I felt I'd been squeezed dry: I'd lost my sap and vinegar. But in 1865, when I lay on my hospital cot, manhood waited to be claimed, like a bag at the freight depot in a city spread out before me like a mirage.

"How old are you, son?" Whitman asked.

"Going on seventeen."

"So young," he said, stroking the back of my hand with his poem-stained fingers. "How did you come to lose your eye?"

I told him the story of my heroism, with embellishments — told it so well, I was nearly persuaded of my exceptional character.

"You sacrificed what little you had to call your own for democracy, freedom, and human dignity. You gave an eye, half of man's greatest blessing, when rich men up north paid a small price to keep themselves and their sons from harm."

With those few words, accompanied by a glance that seemed to measure the dimensions of my meager existence, Whitman made me see myself as a sacrifice on the altar of wealth, but a hero notwithstanding. He didn't believe in tragedy, however; and elbowing me playfully as you would a friend sitting on a bar stool next to yours, he gave me a draught of democratic optimism: He smiled at me with a frankness that, in any race but the American, would have been mistaken for idiocy. The effect was disagreeable, since I'd been enjoying the lugubrious feeling his pity incited in me the way a successful man looks back pleasantly on the privations of his childhood. Their memory is like a drop of Angostura bitters to spice up his gin.

I had yet to develop a conscience — boys rarely have one — and four years of war had blighted what might have taken root in an untroubled season. Hatred and spleen soured me. While I grew, in time, into an ordinary man of equal parts goodness and selfishness, I have a cynic's view of God and His principal creation. My later "visions" confirmed my misanthropy: I've learned that so many of our deeds are really misdeeds committed without thought for the future. I've come to view the world with suspicion and alarm, as even Huck Finn would have, had he seen Tom Sawyer grow into an old man and Jim lynched, his body dumped into the Mississippi.

"You'll be yourself in no time!" Whitman declared with enthusiasm. "The war's nearly finished. The Union has carried the day, and the world's a young man's oyster!" I knew all there was to know about oysters: how they broke your back to harvest, pained your feet to carry from street to street, and lacerated your hands to open. "I'd like to see your Jericho, if you still have it," he said.

I lifted the sheet and showed him my bugle.

He took it up and admired the dents.

"What's your name, friend?"

"Stephen Moran."

"I won't forget you," he said.

Then he gave me his book so that I wouldn't forget *him:* a first edition of *Leaves of Grass,* bound in green cloth. He showed me his picture on the frontispiece, and I saw there the man I'd seen on the beach at Sheepshead Bay and on the streets of New York, jaunty, amused, infatuated with existence — every last sublime and ignoble, gallant and shameful particle of it. All of it, superb!

I carried his book in my haversack, although I wouldn't read it until I got myself jailed and grew homesick for a life that crowds with its multitudes, its noise and smells, its unending parade of being. Whitman's pages shout humanity at you, which is a comfort to the solitary. "I accept Reality," he said, "and dare not question it." Me, I've run from it in horror, just as I once skedaddled from Bull Run. Maybe that explains why I was forever on the move and, for a while, took to living on a train.

"Have you learned to read?" Whitman asked.

"Yes," I said, not in the least insulted.

Most of the boys and many of the men of the 13th Brooklyn were illiterate. Tenement children didn't go to school. But my mother taught me to read from a tattered copy of *Tales, by the O'Hara Family,* which she'd had ever since she was a girl in Dún Laoghaire. Like all her race, she loved stories; and the book, its cloth binding threadbare, was one of the few things left from her days in Ireland. While my father was out boozing, she'd read to me by the stub of a candle, a thread of soot twisting upward from its pinched, meager flame. By her voice alone, she could raise up the old stories from the bones of their words and — lilting between shades of comedy and melodrama — turn the dreary space around me into a stage for the wildest imaginings. That is my happiest recollection of the years in the Bridge Street tenement and of my mother, whose slight body typhoid fever would tint pink and rose like one of Raphael's Madonnas. My brother seems not to have been with us then, although, four years younger than I, he must have been. There is no greater infidelity than memory's desertion.

I thanked Whitman for the book, and he drew down the mosquito netting over me. He may have said I looked like a bride behind the veil, but maybe he didn't. He moved to the next cot to dress the wound of a soldier whose arm was gone. I shut my eye, begrudging the buzzing flies the bedpan they'd appropriated.

Next night, we were awakened by the rumor, whispered down the lane from cot to cot, that Lincoln had been killed. We might have been schoolboys in a dormitory, afraid to give substance to their fears by speaking them aloud, and not sick or maimed soldiers in a hospital ward. Across the mall, on Tenth Street, the lights blazed at every window of the Petersen house, where the good man was not dead but dying into morning from an actor's bullet: Booth's, he who had once played Romeo and Hamlet. The hospital was dark, the gibbous moon low. We couldn't see if the streetlights had been put out in mourning or if the stars were dimmed in grief. The death of Lincoln was high tragedy, and I hope to find the words to say what it meant — never mind their purple. None of us slept. We were silent and timid, as though we ourselves waited for the hearse to come and collect our corpses.

At half past seven in the morning, an officer arrived. Shoulders stooped by the burden of his loss (for each one who loved Lincoln, the loss was unique), he stood next to the washtubs and told us that the president had just died. Tears ran into his cavalry mustache. He wiped them on his sleeve, careless of the fancy braid and buttons. He had relinquished his claim to our respect, paying his own in mourning to his dead commander in chief. I admired him. In a moment, he was gone; but I can recall his face even now. I can't think of that April morning without seeing him — naked and abject as we are when bereft of hope — standing, without the customary iron in his backbone, by the gray washtubs while dismal morning light entered the eastward windows, followed by a breeze that quickened the tar smell of carbolic soap. I closed my eye and saw in my mind's blackness a meteor fall.

Garfield and McKinley would also be assassinated; the death bell would toll for them, too. But Lincoln's murder was the first and cast the longest shadow. For those who suffered the Civil War with him, his life, as well as death, belongs to them. More deaths are bound to follow for as long as some believe the quickest way to change other people's minds is to put a bullet through their brains. But who am I to talk?

I always said that a man made his own bed. But now that I'm dying — there's no point in arguing the fact — now that I am, I realize the futility of struggling against fate. Our bed is made for us: We do as we are obliged. Leastways, enough to humble us. That's a bitter pill to swallow late in the day. While we're alive, we're like a man who steps in horseshit on his way to church. Only when he's home again and has cleaned his shoes can he smile at his humiliation and — more to the point — his helplessness before what lies in wait and is beyond his power to prevent. Here's what I think: Behind every gunman stands another gunman, in a concatenation of death and destruction, difficult to break.

Here's a story: On an afternoon in Santa Fe, when I'd left the mail car to stretch my legs in town, I saw a farmer gunned down by a cattleman. While the dust was soaking up the dead man's blood, the farmer's son picked up his father's gun and shot the cattleman dead — only to be killed, in his turn, by the man's brother. A tired old story, but true nonetheless.

Five days after Lincoln's death, on the twentieth of April, a major attached to the War Department came to the Armory Square Hospital to speak to me.

"You are Private Stephen Moran, bugler in the One Hundred and Seventy-third New York Infantry?" he asked, standing at the foot of my cot.

"Yes, sir." His presence there surprised me. Mine was one of the lowliest ranks and occupations in the army.

"Are you fit to travel?"

"I am, sir."

"Then I ask that you accompany me, Moran."

I put on my uniform and cap and followed the major outside and into a buggy. He drove to the War Department building, next door to the White House, already hung with crepe. There I met Secretary of War Stanton (Lincoln called him "old Mars"), who'd said at the Petersen house when the president slipped into the tide that would carry him into eternity, "Now he belongs to the ages" (or in another version, "angels"). With Stanton was Ulysses S. Grant, adored by every soldier in the Army of the Potomac. My astonishment at seeing the general staggered me, and I rocked unsteadily on my heels. Grant took me by the arm and set me in a chair.

"Are you recovered from your wound, Private?"

"Yes, sir," I said. "You took me by surprise."

Stanton scowled, but Grant seemed pleased by my frankness. He was a man who got on well with his inferiors, who were never made to feel so. And if he liked his whiskey, we didn't hold it against him, being fond of it ourselves.

"Never mind," he said. "I'm just another hardscrabble soldier like yourself."

Stanton snorted. His manner was cold and imperious. Grant, on the other hand, had an urbanity that would have pleased Walt Whitman. Common himself, he appealed to the common soldier. I liked the smell of him, which was of tobacco and the dusty roads we both had traveled, though I never imagined our paths would converge. Captivated by the gold stars on his epaulets, which shone in the excitable light of an April morning, I seemed to have been snared in Lincoln's remarkable destiny, which, with a conspirator's bullet, had entered its tragic phase. But it was vanity for me to think so, and only in his death was I to play a modest part — thanks to Whitman, who had commended my youthful heroism and sacrifice to the secretary of the interior, for whom he worked as a clerk and copyist. Whitman thought a one-eyed bugle boy would add pathos to the mournful spectacle, were he to play taps in the Rotunda, where the president was to lie in state. The secretary mentioned the idea to Stanton, who judged I would be better used, and less likely to offend, by playing my bugle on the rear platform of Lincoln's funeral train as it carried him home to Illinois. I had the impression that, having watched me nearly swoon, Stanton would have returned me forthwith to obscurity, if not for Grant.

"Will you show *him* your devotion one last time?" the general asked, after telling me in the simplest terms why I'd been summoned. He had stressed the word *him,* as if in his mind's eye, the *h* had been a capital letter reserved previously for the Almighty.

I stood and drew myself up to my full height, which at an inch above five feet was hardly impressive, and said in the manliest voice I could muster, "I will, sir!"

Grant beamed down on me, as though he were astride his beloved horse, Cincinnati.

"You won't disgrace us, will you, boy?" said Stanton, with vinegar that could have pickled.

I did not bother to answer him, looking instead at the gray eyes of my general, set in the kindliest of faces.

"He will not," he said, and I knew that I would rather fall on my bugle (I had neither sword nor bayonet) than disappoint him. He saw my resolve and pronounced it "good."

What followed was one of the most remarkable things ever to happen to me. While Stanton grumbled a sort of basso continuo of disapproval, Grant promoted me, then and there, to the rank of sergeant and pinned the Medal of Honor on my blue sack coat.

"It would be unbecoming to the president for you to accompany him to Springfield undecorated," he said.

Saluting him, I bit my tongue as a child

might pinch himself to confirm his presence in the waking world.

Grant returned my salute with a veteran nonchalance and, with a smile of goodwill, dismissed me. (We would never meet again, though he'd help me twice more.) I returned to the hospital, spruced myself up, and exchanged the bandage for the leather eye patch I would wear henceforth. Next morning, I collected my bugle and haversack and walked through the drizzle to the Baltimore & Ohio Depot to await the funeral train's departure.

The wet fields were green with ryegrass and timothy; the willows drooping over the Potomac, the dogwoods, and elm trees called "American" were in leaf. I caught beneath the rain's scent that of the lilac. New lambs foraged the meadows while robins tugged worms from the germinating earth, as on any ordinary April morning. I had seen spring arrive many times before — to battlefields from the Peninsula to Pennsylvania, to the waste grounds of the Five Points and the ash heaps of the Battery. I could not be deceived by Easter promises. The natural world was not opposed to humankind, merely indifferent to it.

Like most of my countrymen, I believed

that we should subdue nature or, failing that, destroy it. According to Genesis, God gave us dominion over the earth and everything that comes of it. On the Great Plains, the army would slaughter buffalo to deprive the Indians of sustenance. Then it would slaughter the Indians. They were in the way of progress and the American meteor, which must fling itself — a blaze of glory — across the Mississippi to the Pacific. After the Washita River massacre and the bone heaps I saw above Bear River, my conscience began to gnaw at me. I wished I could have it out, like tonsils.

At eight o'clock, the train prepared to leave the depot. A framed portrait of Lincoln stood in front of the locomotive's funnel, from which sparks showered into the morning air as the engine overcame its reluctance. On so portentous a day, one might have scried the future in the embers, but I could not. Foreknowledge wouldn't be granted to me until later, near the Little Bighorn.

Washington City to Springfield, Illinois, April 21–May 4, 1865

Mostly, I remember rain. It was an ordinary rain — signifying nothing — produced by whatever agency causes rain to fall; and it fell according to laws governing natural phenomena. That is to say, there was nothing in the least unnatural about it, although it interfered with the enjoyment I took, standing on the rear platform, adorned with my new medal and stripes.

I thought myself an exceptional young man when I raised Jericho to my lips and blew ardently while the train slowed to let country people gawk. In the big cities en route to Springfield, I played my bugle while Mr. Lincoln's coffin was taken off the train and laid on a fancy hearse. I admit I swaggered behind the catafalque drawn by black-plumed horses, between mobs of mourners, down the main streets of Baltimore, Harrisburg, Philadelphia, New York City, Albany, Buffalo, Cleveland, Columbus, Indianapolis, Michigan City, Chicago, and Springfield. In twelve days, the nine funeral cars of the so-called Lincoln Special traveled, in slow and lugubrious procession, one thousand six hundred and fifty-four miles of railroad track, past four hundred and forty-four towns and cities.

I was a fair-haired, clean-shaven, well-turned-out young man, and I swear the girls did not know whether to look at me or the coffin. I carried Jericho under my arm, though I did not perform at the viewings.

Buglers attached to the honor guards of the cities where we stopped played. I could have done just as well as they, but the twin vanities of politics and civic pride were against me. To tell the truth, which I can do more readily now that I am beyond temptation, I was secretly glad. I feared my hand would shake in front of the tens and hundreds of thousands of mourners lined up in their black hats and clothes to see the dead man's face. They knew in their bones, wearied by many hours' waiting, that this occasion, however somber, would be one to lord over those who missed it. They'd have put a pen into Lincoln's hand if they thought he might, by galvanism or sympathy, give them his autograph. You know what people are like.

In recollection, the cities where we stopped run together, but I vividly recall Cleveland, where a reporter and a photographer from the *Cleveland Morning Leader* were assigned to do a piece about the "The Bugler of Five Forks and the Lincoln Special." I have it yet: two columns and a steel engraving of me holding Jericho against my Union coat, next to the Medal of Honor — my eye, caught in the coruscation of the magnesium flash, appearing wide and startled. I would have preferred a brave, unblinking look; nevertheless, I was pleased. Ever since childhood, I'd known that perfection is not of this world and, in all likelihood, not of the next. I was full of myself, my head turned by meeting General Grant and by my shiny decoration. No matter that I deserved neither honor. Or maybe I did, for having suffered sixteen years on this godforsaken planet. My emergence from obscurity had been abrupt. Like an owl surprised in a dark corner of the barn, I was dazzled by the unexpected light. But it didn't last; neither my celebrity nor vainglory lasted much beyond Springfield, where Lincoln and his son Willie were carried to their rest on a gaudy silver-gold-and-crystal hearse lent by the city of St. Louis. Twelve years later, thieves were caught stealing Lincoln's coffin, intending to ransom his remains for the release of the infamous Ben Boyd, jailed for counterfeiting. You know what people are like. I always did. In my life, I was never disillusioned — never lost my innocence, for I had none to start with.

Chicago was memorable for the Irish laundress who gave me the eye, or maybe I gave her mine, as I walked behind the hearse, pulled by eight black horses down Michigan Avenue toward the courthouse. I left the procession and joined her at the curb. She was my age or a little younger — pretty in the way of colleens everywhere, although her face and hands looked boiled. I'd seen enough of her kind to know that in ten years she'd lose her prettiness to steam and lye. She wasn't in the least bashful, having the flippant manner of the Irish, who — they are quick to tell you — are no worse, or better, than anyone else except the Negroes. I liked her and reached out to touch her mouth; she bit my finger and laughed.

"You're a bold one," she said, "to be taking liberties with a young girl. I'll call a copper if you try that on me again."

I fingered my medal, picked at a thread on the sergeant's stripes, and gave her what I judged to be a worldly, contemptuous look. She must have seen it before, because she sneered. My dignity collapsed and, with it, the pretense of her annoyance. She took my arm and led me down a side street to a tenement hardly distinguishable from the one I'd left in Brooklyn four years before. Except for an old woman who coughed unmercifully on the other side of the wall separating the girl's room from hers, the building was empty of people — all gone to see Mr. Lincoln's send-off. Her room was little better than a closet, containing the runt half of a trundle bed, a pinewood bureau, and a lyre-backed chair. Outside, scarcely visible through the dirty window, was an alleyway jammed with barrels of rubbish and ash, beneath clotheslines hung with wash that didn't look quite clean.

The girl — I don't remember her name, if I ever knew it — unpinned her hat, set it on the chair, and then, unpinning her hair, shook down a glossy tumble of chestnut. I buried my face in it, as if it might contain the remedy for an uneasy heart. I suppose mine was that, although I'd hardly stopped long enough since my flight from Brooklyn to have noticed. Pitying myself, I felt like crying but undid the buttons of her blouse instead.

I'd like to boast how, confident and suave, I swept her into ecstasy. But the fact of the matter is, I fumbled and made a shambles of love. She was my first — I don't count what'd happened in the chaplains' hut — and I was bound to be clumsy and afraid. She knew more than I about the convergence of the sexes. She helped me through my ordeal, and never once did she make me feel ashamed. But I was, and with our comedy ended, I hurriedly dressed and ran out into the street to lick my wounds and compose the story of my conquest: one I'd tell often, in conjunction with that of my heroism at Five Forks, in saloons, freight yards, and at railheads. Such fabrications are common among men — and among women, too, for all I know of them.

I retraced my steps down Michigan Avenue, moving against the tide of mourners on their way to view the Rail Splitter's remains. I passed beneath a banner strung across the street, proclaiming, THE HEAVENS ARE DRAPED IN BLACK. I remember the rain, although maybe it was only in my mind that it fell. I do recall having heard the courthouse bell toll all the way to Lake Michigan, where the president's train had stopped on a length of track thrown over the water on a trestle. Moved by the melancholy bell, I took Jericho and, standing on the funeral car's rear platform, blew taps — not for Lincoln, but for my own pathetic self. I don't believe I ever played it better. Lincoln freed three million slaves, but I couldn't free even so measly a thing as Stephen Moran. I wish I could tell you that a meteor fell into Lake Michigan, but it didn't.

We left Chicago for Springfield, riding through the night on the St. Louis & Alton tracks. Sleepless, I sat up with the president and Willie, who'd died of typhoid three years earlier. He had been disinterred from the Georgetown cemetery so that he might spend the silent ages with his father. Fort Wayne Junction, Bridgeport, Summit, Joy's, Lemont, Lockport, Joliet (where twelve thousand mourners gathered at midnight in a silent sea of stricken faces and bared heads), Elwood, Hampton, Wilmington, Stewart's Grove, Braceville, Gardner, Dwight, Odell, Cayuga, Pontiac, Ocoya, Chenoa, Lexington, Towanda, Bloomington, Shirley, Funk's Grove, McLean, Atlanta, Lawn Dale, Lincoln, Broadwell, Elkhart, Williamsville, Sherman Station, Sangamon — towns and hamlets passed before my burning eye in a blur of faces made terrible by the wavering lights of kerosene lamps and torches.

I feared I would vomit because of the smell of decomposition, noticeable in the parlor car ever since New York City, in spite of the onboard embalmer's diligence. The president's face, visible through the small hatch on the coffin's lid, was turning black — a sign for those who took an interest in such things. I supposed it was for reason of the odor that I, among all living men and women aboard the train, had the car to myself that night. Remembering the cigars

Grant had left for me, I lit one, wondering if he'd known I'd have need of it. I meant no disrespect by my fumigation, and I felt certain that Mr. Lincoln, who had understood expediency, would have forgiven me mine, had he been able to render a posthumous judgment.

I suppose it only natural that I thought of Grant while enjoying one of his cigars. Of all the men I'd known, he was the best — even better than the man the world called "Honest Abe." The vicious called him "Ape" and other hateful names. Neither man could abide pomp or fuss, but Grant was a rough soldier and the general who'd as good as anointed me with the flat of his sword on that April morning in 1865, at the beginning of my westering. He did much that was good besides: enforced the civil rights of former slaves and sent troops against the Klan. Sadly, the war against the buffalo, the Lakota Sioux, and the Cheyenne would take the shine off my admiration. Black Friday, the Whiskey Ring, the Delano affair — the scandalous history of his administration didn't concern me.

New York . . . I suppose I ought to tell what happened there, though I behaved shamefully.

In New York, sixteen horses pulled the coffin on an opulent funeral car. I left the parade up Broadway to see if I might happen upon my father in one of the barrooms he used to haunt. But they were closed, their windows shuttered, so that even Manhattan's most heroic drunkards were obliged to abstain for a day of mourning. As I turned away from the locked door of the Dragon's Blood, frequented by men of the printing trade, a man stepped toward me and thrust a card into my hand. I had seen him earlier, skulking on the pavement that the mob deserted once the cortege had passed on its way to Fourteenth Street. Engraved and bordered in black, the stiff card resembled those used to announce a death in the family. It bore, in Cooper Italic, the motto *Sic Semper Tyrannis.* Knowing no Latin, I couldn't decipher it. I thanked him — a small, furtive man in a greasy frockcoat — and put the card in my wallet. He clapped me on the back and shook my hand; I did the same to him.

"You look like a man with a mighty thirst," he said.

"I could stand a glass or two of beer," I replied.

"The saloons are closed for the 'Great Emancipator's' funeral," he said in a tone of voice I thought a trifle snide. "I happen to know a private club where we can drink a great man's health for freedom's sake."

"Sounds fine to me," I said.

He led me down Broadway and into an alley, at the end of which was an engraver's establishment. He rapped on the door in a complicated staccato, as though he meant to raise a spirit in the next world. We were let inside by a fat man decidedly of this one. The light was bad; the dreary shop smelled of acid and chemicals. The walls were papered over haphazardly with engravings of every sort: animals of the veldt, wildflowers of the Great Plains, the pyramids at Giza, pugilists in old New York, a patent medicine catalog. The floor, too, was littered with inked foolscap, stamped in grime by the soles of hobnailed boots.

We followed the fat man into a cleaner, more spacious and illuminated room, where half a dozen others sat around a table laid with bottles of Tennessee whiskey and lager, as well as plates of pickled pigs' feet, onions, and herring. We sat down, and I helped myself to beer and herring, while the man who'd brought me — his name, I think, was Titus — gave his impressions of the spectacle, which the others evidently had ignored. I went on to sample the whiskey and the pigs' feet, paying slight attention to the talk around me. The more I drank, the less I was able to take in what was said, but I had a notion that the men spoke insultingly of the dead president. I wanted to object, to stand on my dignity and rebuke them for their irreverence, but the whiskey had tied my tongue, and I could hardly stand without toppling — never mind my dignity. So, feeling there was nothing to be done, I downed another glass.

"Let's drink a toast to our Great Emancipator," the fat man said. "To him who, with a single bullet, has delivered us from the tyrant."

They raised their glasses to a framed engraving of John Wilkes Booth, shrouded in crepe.

"Sic Semper Tyrannis!" they shouted in unison. "Thus Ever to Tyrants!"

They eyed me suspiciously. Pickled as I was, I sensed their anger brewing, hot and bitter. I felt like Caesar encircled by the conspirators, with no place to duck.

"Why aren't you toasting him?" asked a man who'd been introduced to me as a retired expediter for the slave trade.

He was red-faced, potbellied, and wheezing. He reminded me of Mr. Fezziwig, whose picture I'd seen while thumbing through a book left out on a major's bunk.

That was during the do-nothing days before Bull Run, when McClelland liked to play soldiers. I've never known a cockier son of a bitch than McClelland. Can you imagine if he'd beaten Lincoln in '64? Old Abe's life would have been spared, but the country would have gone to hell.

"Perhaps you mistook him for a sympathizer," growled a fierce old Copperhead.

"He shook my hand when I gave him the card," Titus replied indignantly, nodding toward a stack of them on the table. "He laid it in his wallet, like a lock of his sweetheart's hair."

"He's a damned Yankee sergeant!" snarled a weak-eyed, ink-stained man with the shape and color of a carrot. "You must've been crazy to bring him here!"

"Plenty of Federal boys hate Lincoln for putting them through hell for the sake of the niggers!" Titus spluttered, like fire falling on damp tinder.

"What's that medal he's wearing? For murdering Confederate boys, I suppose!" barked an Arkansas man who claimed to have mailed Lincoln seventeen death threats since '64: one for each year of life taken, by a Union hangman, from the "Boy Martyr of the Confederacy," David Owen Dodd.

I pretended to have fallen asleep. They shook me roughly awake to explain myself.

"Let him kiss the stick!" Titus said. "That'll prove it one way or the other."

A skinny red-haired man named Gaiter, who'd lost a fortune in cotton during the war, fetched the stick while Titus praised it, for my benefit, as the one that hotheaded South Carolina Congressman Preston Brooks had used to beat the abolitionist Charles Sumner "to within an inch of his damned life" on the Senate floor. Gaiter handled it with reverence, as you would a relic of a Christian saint. He offered it to my lips, and I kissed it willingly enough. There was room on the calendar for only one martyrdom in April, and my erstwhile commander in chief was welcome to it. I was, remember, just sixteen years of age and enfeebled by strong drink.

My show of adoration appeased them. They clapped me on the back and filled my glass, but when I commenced to vomit up a swill of pigs' feet and whiskey with a chaser, they hurried me outside and slammed the door. I considered myself fortunate to have escaped with my life. They were ridiculous but dangerous notwithstanding. Was I a coward? Would you have lit the fuse and waited to be hoisted by your own petard?

Often, I'd measure myself against other men and find myself wanting in courage, in selflessness, in any kind of love.

I'd never again go looking for my father. In fact, that day in New York City, the twenty-fifth of April, would be nearly my last back east. I'd make one more excursion there, ten, eleven years later. Increasingly, I would come to feel the tug of the West. It wasn't anything definite. I had no tiny Horace Greeley in my head, urging me in that direction. It was a feeling, a sense, a raw emotion that stole over me, like rye whiskey taken slow. If westering was America's destiny, it was also mine.

The sweetish odor of animal corruption assailed my nose, snapping my reverie in two. My cigar had gone out. Lighting it, I saw in its glowing ember the dead leaves in the thickets of the Spotsylvania Wilderness that our musket lints had set ablaze. They burned down a stand of trees and, in it, hundreds of trapped Federal soldiers. That was Grant's worst day of the war, and also theirs.

On the morning of May the third, twelve days after having left Washington, Mr. Lincoln reached the end of his journey — unless you believe in the lessons of the Sunday school — at the Chicago & Alton Depot on

Jefferson Street. I had thousands of miles yet to travel. They took him and Willie to the State House, where, with rouge chalk and amber, the undertaker made *our* Great Emancipator's face presentable. The day scorched, as though hell's own wind were loosed on Springfield to mock him; and I feared that the secret processes of the embalmer's art would be undone. I nearly shouted, because of the heat and my anxiousness, that they should hurry the dead man to his tomb and slam the heavy door shut to prevent some horror. Nerves strung tight like piano wire, I felt I was a player in an ancient tragedy. Was this how Booth felt on that Good Friday in Washington? Had he absorbed too much of *Julius Caesar,* in which he'd played Marc Antony to his brother's Brutus? It ought to have been the other way round, but things are seldom so neatly done in real life. (Was my life real? Real and unreal, like everybody else's. Photographers can get muddled up in that kind of question — the serious ones can.)

At the cemetery the next day, the feeling that I was extraordinary, that I was a person at the center of great events left me. Modesty prevailed, an unfamiliar emotion to one who liked to show off. I didn't push ahead of the others standing at the iron door of the tomb; I skulked among the trees. I'd had enough of celebrity. I was sorry for Father Abraham, for me, for the whole damned world. Of Bishop Simpson's interminable oration, I remember only this: "His moral power gave him preeminence." I walked back to the railroad depot, thinking how I might acquire such power. I felt full of a great and noble purpose. By the next day, I'd forgotten all about it.

Springfield, Illinois, May 26–December 7 (Thanksgiving Day), 1865

In Springfield, I shot a man named Jacob Lowry. He came at me with a bayonet he claimed to have used to gut the blue bellies at Chickamauga. I stood in the street and called him a scavenger of corpses belonging to honorable men — in blue and gray — cut down in battles he was too scared to fight. I don't know which side of the truth I'd landed on in my ire. It didn't matter, because the reason he lunged at me with that tarnished piece of steel had nothing to do with the War of Secession, but with a pretty black-haired girl. Funny, I can remember Lowry's name but not hers. Fury must be a stronger, more durable emotion than — call it "infatuation," since I'm not sure I ever understood love.

I was at loose ends after Mr. Lincoln was laid to rest. With no money or place to go, I took a job at a feed and grain store in Springfield. Lincoln's parlor car was sold to the Union Pacific Railroad, but I was allowed to sleep there until a train heading to Nebraska Territory could be made up. A girl — she was eighteen and filled her bodice handsomely — came into the store one morning for a bushel of dried corn. I had on my blue coat and — I'm embarrassed to admit — the Medal of Honor. It must have impressed her, unless it was something in my face she liked. The workings of a woman's heart and mind are mysterious to me.

We began to see each other. She showed me what respectable amusements the town had to offer: dances in the grange and church halls, baseball games, picnics and band concerts by the Sangamon River, and walks along its bluffs. I taught her euchre and keno, games I'd learned while soldiering. I held her hand and mooned over her. I might've kissed her. It's a shame if I didn't — she was a pretty girl. We walked out together from late May until Thanksgiving, when Lowry returned to Springfield. He'd been in Charleston after Sherman thrashed it with fire and sword. Lowry was like a magpie picking at leftover stubble in hopes of finding shiny trash. Now, once again in town, he let it be known that he had an understanding with the girl and no Federal son of a bitch was going to trespass on his territory.

"We had no such thing, Jacob!" she scolded, after he'd barged into the kitchen and laid claim to her. We had just sat down with her mother and young brother to eat our Thanksgiving turkey.

"You're a lying bitch!" he screamed.

"I could never stand the sight or smell of you!" she screamed right back.

His unsavory presence in the close kitchen confirmed her low opinion of him. In a fury of resentment, he cut her lip with the back of his hand and tried to kick my chair out from under me with his muddy boot. Her mother jumped up with a napkin to staunch her daughter's bloody mouth. The boy began to whimper. The dog, waiting underneath the table for carelessness and gravity to serve him dinner, yelped. I sank the carving fork into Lowry's thigh. He pulled it out and flung it at me, but his aim was poor, doubtless owing to the pain. I laughed as he hobbled in a rage out the kitchen door.

"You'll wish you was in hell, boy, when I get done with you!" he shouted from the yard.

My insides were quivering like a custard, but I managed a show of gallantry worthy of my medal. Who's to say who is or is not deserving of his honors?

The widow — her husband had been killed at Shiloh — went into the front room and began to mangle "Rock Me Back to Sleep, Mother" on an upright piano. The boy shared a turkey leg with the dog. I had lost my appetite for dinner and romance and was about to say good night when the girl — I wish I could remember her name! — disappeared into an unlit room. I thought, for a moment, that she meant me to follow her and receive in the discreet darkness my reward for having sent her suitor packing. I waited in confusion, listening to a drawer groan open and shut. In another moment, she returned to the kitchen with a Colt pistol.

"It was my daddy's. I've kept it cleaned and oiled," she said proudly.

I looked at it as if it were the turkey's other leg.

"You best be careful," she said, touching my eye patch wistfully. "Jake's got it in for you, and he was crazy even before he went away to fight."

Reluctantly, I accepted the pistol; its cold, sobering weight annulled the evening's farce, just as John Wilkes Booth's derringer had turned a frivolous *Our American Cousin* into tragedy.

I was no gunman; my talent was musical. Depressed, I opened the back door, stepped into the yard, and turned. Standing in the doorway with the skittish light behind her, she kissed me. The moment comes back to me in a rush of recollection: how I turned to take her hand in mine — the one holding the Colt — and then stammered an apology for my clumsiness. Pleased by my confusion (proof of her fascination), she kissed me lightly on the mouth. I tasted blood like a rusty spoon. She shut the door on me. The windowpanes were wet inside the kitchen, where the stove was roaring against the December cold — unless it was my ears that roared.

I walked back to the depot in the "mystical moist night-air," careless of danger, thinking only of how I might taste her kiss again, so easily was a young man satisfied in that — I nearly said "innocent time." But there was nothing innocent about that time — not when it came to lives cut short, hobbled, or robbed of painlessness. Boys may have been barely acquainted with sex, but they were on familiar terms with dying. Even a fraudulent bugle boy would already have seen death in its ingenious masks and bewildering variety of postures, all of them perfect for the long-held gaze of Matthew Brady and his tribe.

I lay awake in the funeral car, the Colt on the nightstand — my head spinning with ragtag thoughts. I remembered Philadelphia, where the funeral train had stopped at Broad Street Station on its way to New York. That night, there was to be a private viewing at Independence Hall.

Philadelphia, Pennsylvania, April 22, 1865

I wandered down Market Street to the Delaware, where a young Ben Franklin had arrived from Boston with only a Dutch dollar and a copper shilling to his name. On the wharf that afternoon, I felt that I, too, might yet make something of my life. In the broad brown river that, from instant to instant, was discharging its measureless potential in unceasing motion, I sensed a like potential in me, not entirely wasted by my sixteen years as a ne'er-do-well. Life — the better part of it — lay before me, as it had for Franklin, just off the Boston packet. I can still do something, I told myself; and then I tripped over a stern line stretched tight around a bollard by the outbound tide and fell headlong into the river. I couldn't swim, had never learned the art, though I'd been terrified of drowning while I raked up oysters or stole rides on the Brooklyn ferry.

Delivered, finally, unto the water, I was all for drowning. To hell with Ben Franklin — the game wasn't worth the candle. I felt a languor stealing over me as my body began to tire. It had resisted the river's lap — so amorous and inviting — in spite of me. Then, when words like *will, desire, resignation* had lost their meaning, I was hauled out with the abruptness of a fish taken from its element. I woke — it was like waking — to a man busily rowing my arms to rid me of river water. Lying on the planked bottom of a skiff, I coughed and stared at the white sun overhead.

"You all right, boy?" he asked.

He was a colored man of middle age. We'd have called him worse back then. Many still would. The look of concern on his face seemed genuine.

I took my time in answering him, nostalgic for the numbness through which I'd recently passed on my way to elsewhere or nowhere. I blinked my eyes awhile, fidgeted, and wriggled in the noonday light. I knew I ought to thank him, and in a moment I did — convincingly, it seemed to me.

"Yes. Thanks, mister," I said, fixing my eye patch, which had been skewed by the current.

He tied up to the wharf, collected his fishing pole and creel, and then followed behind me as I climbed the ladder to the dock. He lived nearby and insisted I go home with him to dry my clothes. It seemed the sensible thing, and I did as he asked. I felt squeamish about going inside a black man's house. But I went — maybe to prove to myself I was a different boy from the one who'd fallen into the river. Maybe I wanted to believe I'd been changed by my "Baptist drowning." The lies we tell ourselves!

He gave me a shirt and a much-mended pair of pants, which I put on willingly to show I had no prejudice. He made me drink hot broth while I sat in front of the fire, in his front room. He handled my uniform respectfully, as you would a priest's Sunday outfit, wringing the blue coat and pants with his strong black hands before hanging them up to dry. He wanted to know what I was doing in Philadelphia. I told him I had arrived that morning on the Lincoln Special, with the president's body.

"I ought to have done nothing all day,

except pray for Uncle Abe," he said sheepishly. "But I suppose he won't mind, seeing as how Jesus Himself liked to fish."

I allowed that he was right.

"Mr. Lincoln freed me," he said. "I owe him my life."

His voice was pitched between pride and resentment. I didn't understand why he should feel the latter but decided it was none of my business. Besides, I was too busy considering my destiny, which seemed, more and more, to be the work of powerful influences.

Once again, I felt I'd gotten tangled in a knot of unusual convergences, whose threads included Whitman, Grant, Lincoln, Franklin, and now this black man — his name was Spotswood — whose heart was just as unfathomable. I knew nothing of his suffering or sorrows. They were likely to be heavier and harder to bear than mine, though I had suffered and sorrowed some. The room bore not a trace of a past or present life: no pictures on the walls, no gimcracks or souvenirs. It appeared to have been scrubbed clean of remembrance. I almost asked to hear his story but decided it would be inconsiderate of me and maybe painful for him.

We had been talking of this and that, the

way strangers will when their lives momentarily converge. When darkness entered the room, we fell silent. Spotswood lit two candles, and we sat together in the deepening night, the ceiling thatched with shadows. I think he was keeping a vigil for the man whose body lay a few blocks to the west, where the Liberty Bell, like him, was broken and mute. To tell the God's honest truth, I don't know what thoughts might have been chasing one another round in Spotswood's brain. My own were none too clear. I strained to keep my mind centered on Lincoln, but it wandered elsewhere: to Brooklyn and my mother's grave, Five Forks and the Armory Square Hospital, Walt Whitman and oysters.

I wanted Spotswood to remember me — God knows why. I told him my name several times. I would have written it down if there'd been a pencil. I wished I had some little gift to make him in honor of our encounter and the entanglement of our two lives. He'd saved mine, after all. Maybe I was just glad to have been born a white man. And for the first time in my life, I was glad to have been born in Brooklyn! Supposing I'd been reared up in the South, the son of a plantation owner. What would have become of me? Very possibly, I'd have died, or been put in a prison cell next to Jeff Davis's, or hanged like Captain Wirz, commandant of Andersonville, who let thirteen thousand Union men perish. And where would I be now? Damned, most likely. Strange the ways of fate, as the saying goes. This fact might interest you, Jay: The pistol with which Booth shot Lincoln dead was made in Philadelphia by the gunsmith Henry Derringer. And there I was, in Philadelphia, dressed in clothes belonging to a slave freed by the dead man I was escorting to his final and lasting repose. Yes, I had a destiny all right. Like it or not.

My clothes dry, I dressed and thanked Spotswood for his kindness with what I believe was genuine warmth, taking his black hand and holding it in mine — the same hand that would hold a Springfield girl's and also put a bullet into the forehead of hateful Jake Lowry. The hand, you know, was shaped for murder and for love.

Springfield, Illinois, December 8, 1865–January 14, 1866

The day following the Thanksgiving debacle, I woke, feeling grainy-eyed and irritable from too little sleep. I dressed in my uniform, pinned on my medal, and walked down Jefferson Street to the eatery where I took my breakfast. I dawdled over my eggs, thinking of the Colt pistol in my waistband and what the advertisement claimed: "Abe Lincoln may have freed all men, but Sam Colt made them equal." I didn't feel equal to anybody, except for old Spotswood. I was always subject to mental vicissitudes: the highs and lows of a mind inadequately moored. It must have made me a difficult person to get along with, which may explain why I spent the greater part of my life alone. But that was my way, and nobody can help his way.

"Snow coming," said the grizzled counterman to break the silence. He wore a damp dish towel across his shoulder with the panache of a diplomat or a Mexican bandit. He gave me a meaningful look. "This afternoon or maybe tonight."

I nodded, unwilling to discourse on the subject of weather, good or bad. I had things on my mind. But so as not to get a reputation for being standoffish and superior, I beamed at him before returning to my scrambled eggs. He coughed, as if to introduce a further elaboration. I fixed my eye on the end of my fork, refusing to be drawn in. A woman entered, making the bell above the door hop, and ordered fried potatoes for her husband, laid up after a hod of bricks had fallen on him. I felt safe for the moment from distraction.

Ambition was not yet among my virtues. Or is it a vice? I'd aspired to nothing, striven for nothing, envied no man his good fortune or lot in life. My desires had been modest enough to make me a Christian example of temperance. Or a Hindu one, for that matter. Religions look very much the same, once you scrape off the crust. God is everywhere, unless He is nowhere. But I believed myself to be in love with this Springfield girl. Taking stock, I had little to offer her. The feed and grain store didn't pay much. I managed to make ends meet only because I was living gratis in the funeral car. Even if it weren't soon be on its way to Omaha, I couldn't expect a young bride to take up residence where two bodies had ripened into corruption, no matter how famous their former owners. When the fire's gone out, a leper is the equal of a king — and vice versa — death being the one true democracy. Until my prospects improved, I couldn't expect to marry her.

How could I have forgotten the name of someone so dear to me? Unless I'd mistaken my feelings. What did I know of love? What do I know of it now? Heartbreak. Heartbreak and a misery — that's what love is. But what if the confidences I've received in the whiskey-scented confessionals of barrooms, barracks, and backwater depots down the years from love's besotted, disappointed, jilted, and abused victims are untrue? What if love is really what the poets say of it? I don't feel equal to the subject. Desire, maybe; the reckless passions that scald without warmth or tenderness, certainly. But not love. Of this, I felt sure even then. I pushed a strip of bacon cased in congealed fat around my plate, feeling once more in the trough of the wave, waiting for momentum to lift me up. Disgusted, I slapped a few coins on the table, wiped my mustache, and left.

Tomas Bergman, who owned the business, had gone to Lake Springfield for the ice fishing, as he did each year when the water froze. Except for a half-deaf old black man who hauled feed sacks in and out of the barn, I was alone in the store. Customers would be few on the day after Thanksgiving. Dog-tired, I lay down on a shelf behind the counter and slept. I dreamed, I suppose; but I'll be damned if I can remember what. No, I won't make up a dream simply to round out my story. While I might not be interested in history, except for the parts I clambered through, I'd like to tell the truth, insofar as I am able and inasmuch as it can be told. Funny, how I'd come to believe the fabrication concerning the loss of my eye!

Spotswood had said that to start again was impossible; that all we could do was wait. He didn't say for what, nor did he say why we couldn't begin anew. I should have asked, but the twilight that had brought out in him a strain of melancholy befuddled me and turned my tongue to India rubber. Night came and silenced him with gloomy thoughts: of Honest Abe, perhaps, stretched out inside his trestled coffin, or of some private, embittering grief that caused a portion of him to despise Lincoln, me, and the entire white race. Yet, I'd seen him touch my uniform the way someone would Jesus' robe or shroud. Maybe an old slave's habit of ingratiation remained in him, stubborn and ineradicable. No, he was not so devious a man. I wish I could have seen into his heart, which, like everyone else's, was shut. I sometimes wonder if I see truly into my own.

A chicken farmer from out by Riverton came in and stamped snow off his boots, leaving two wet puddles to dry as he walked to the counter and rang the little brass bell. Jolted, I slunk out of my roost and onto the floor behind the counter and pretended to be counting scuttles.

"Yes, sir," I said, getting to my feet. "What can I do for you?"

He placed his order, scratched a raspy cheek, in a few words commented on the snow falling generally over the county, and left the store — satisfied he had done neither more nor less than he was obliged by the social contract, whose ghost is felt by all men and women, even the meanest who flout it. In a world of strangers, this rough chicken farmer was determined not to stand out from the rest. Thus are we ever to one another, and alone. Like Grant in the midst of his army, like Lincoln in his White House, like my father with his bottle, like my brother in an alleyway, surrounded by roughnecks who would break his neck for their profit or pleasure, like Ben Franklin with his pennies and his loaves of bread when he arrived in Philadelphia to start afresh, and like Spotswood, who had emptied his house and was waiting in the failing light for whatever would come next.

I went outside to the barn to give the old man the feed order and found him asleep on a pile of sacks. I kicked him twice.

"Wake up, you lazy bastard!"

He opened his revolting old eyes and looked at me with unmistakable contempt, so that I had to kick him again. His eyes reminded me of ropy strands of egg white and bloody yolks. I wanted to scramble them with my fist. I don't know why I should have felt such ill will, except that I'd overheard him tell the black kid who swept the place how I was a conceited jackass to wear my uniform and medal when I wasn't a soldier anymore. I didn't much care for his remark. I hate to think that I had a vindictive streak in those days, but I guess it's true. If he were here, I'd ask his forgiveness; but he was no doubt shoveled rudely into the colored cemetery long ago.

I gave him the chicken farmer's order for dried corn and left him to his hard work and chilly barn. I walked back over my tracks, now nearly obliterated by the falling snow. I flung some coal into the stove and sat on the high stool, going over things in my mind. As the room grew hot, I felt a momentary pang of remorse and almost went back to the barn to invite the old man inside to get warm. But I didn't. Instead, I worried over the girl, the poor showing I must make in her eyes, my unused potential glimpsed on a wharf in Philadelphia, and my empty days. I had forgotten all about Lowry's dire threat.

I closed early because of the snow, which

sat on the railings and sills and leaned against the walls. The sky was white with it. Indifferent, I'd wintered in worse: in Pennsylvania with the regiment and in Brooklyn as a boy when the wind would drive snow into our room through a broken pane of glass. In winter, a tenement is a cold and inhospitable place. I walked down the middle of Fifth, fairly cleared by streetcars and wagons of the powdery snow. A block shy of Jefferson Street, Lowry bolted from a tobacconist's doorway, where he'd been lying in ambush, having scouted my route from Bergman's to the depot. He flung himself on me, accompanied by the shrill, unholy rebel yell, which had caused many a Yankee soldier to dampen his blue pants. I shot him down with the Colt before he could stick me with his bayonet.

The tobacconist, whose testimony was tainted by his friendship with Lowry, which he naturally denied, told the Springfield police that Lowry had gone out to speak to me about our differences. He'd kept his distance, he hadn't yelled, and the bayonet had stayed tucked up in his belt. He swore I'd called Lowry names no man could tolerate, and then — "entirely without provocation and in cold blood" — I'd drawn my pistol, aimed, and shot him through the forehead. There might have been a morsel of truth in what he said, but Lowry had had no cause to jump me the way he did.

I remember the squeak of my boots on dry snow, the slap of my rubber coat, the creak of hinges on the tobacconist's door, the snap of a tree branch, the rasp of my lungs drawing breath, and, after a curious sigh, the rattle of Lowry's lungs just before he crumpled and fell.

Had I been an ordinary young man, doubtless I would have been tried as a cold-blooded killer, convicted, and taken in chains to Leavenworth to break rocks for twenty or thirty years. But I had been presented with the Medal of Honor by Ulysses S. Grant himself for my valor at Five Forks and had been handpicked by the secretary of war to serve in Abraham Lincoln's honor guard. I could not be easily swept under the judicial carpet and left to rot among the dust weevils. I was a special case. It was decided I would remain in the city jail until the Lincoln parlor car departed Springfield for Omaha, with me on it. Banished like a medieval prince, I could never again set foot in Illinois.

While I waited for the Union Pacific to take the car away (is this what Spotswood had meant by "waiting"?), I wondered if my celebrity — the case had been a spectacle for some, a scandal for others — impressed the girl. She might be willing to share my exile. She might not be bothered by the parlor car's morbid associations. Originally, it had been built as a sort of democratic triumphal car for the president to confer with his generals in the field and to see for himself the results of their campaigns. Fit for a pasha, it was too splendid for modest Old Abe, who in his lifetime had refused to use it. He could hardly do so in death, the commemoration of which would have embarrassed him by its extravagance. When he traveled to Gettysburg to deliver his address, he rode in a train such as anyone would take on a mundane journey to a commonplace destination. Death, however — its kingdom or realm — required a stylish conveyance. Mr. Lincoln's funeral car was comfortable and smart. It had the makings of a bridal bower of bliss. The girl ought to jump at the chance to marry me. Such were the idiocies that passed through my feverish brain.

The girl faithfully visited me in my cell, once: to give me a newly baked apple pie and a letter, written in an awkwardly childish hand, informing me of her decision — before I'd so much as asked for one — to have nothing further to do with me because of the "shame and disgrace." For the rest of her life, she wrote, she would regret the kiss she'd bestowed on me in a moment of pity. Galled, I swore to forget her and looked forward to putting ten or twenty years between us. The months spent in Springfield had been a disaster for me. Maybe if I'd dwelled on poor Lincoln's cold dwindling inside his tomb, I wouldn't have been such a damned fool. Remorse always comes late in the day.

Bored, lonely, and sorry for myself, I took Whitman's book from my haversack. I stared at its green cover, scuffed and stained by time. Even a few months will leave its traces, provided they are packed with life. While I perused his catalog of humankind, my cell grew crowded with every type of man and woman, clamoring and jostling or nonchalant and imperturbable. I relished their stink and noise. In his *Song of Myself* (so unlike my braying), Whitman seemed like Christ. I'd have said "Buddha," had I not been ignorant of any belief except my own. My faith in God and in his creatures may have been weak — a rope frayed to its breaking point by the strain of a small, mean, knockabout life — but I'd heard stories of a gentle Jesus from my mother. In my cell, I remembered how Whitman had leaned over my hospital cot to console me for my wound. I'd have given him my blessing, gladly, had he sauntered through the prison door, hooked his arm around my neck, and called me "comrade." Of the poems (if that's what they are) I read in jail, I recall this:

> I am possess'd!
> Embody all presences outlaw'd or suffering,
> See myself in prison shaped like another man . . .

I waited five weeks for the train that would take the parlor car and me to Omaha. Maybe in Nebraska, I thought. Maybe on the other side of the Mississippi, I'll find my own song. If there's one to be found.

Omaha, Nebraska Territory, January 15, 1866–October 19, 1866

We should count ourselves lucky that Lincoln's funeral car got sold to a railroad instead of a traveling freak show. Can you picture it, Jay: the "World's Tallest Man" tucked up in Abe's extra-long bed while pinheads gawk at themselves in the ornate mirrors? Our century didn't value sentiment unless it was gold-leafed inside a Valentine. Remember the calendars put out by the packinghouses, illustrated with lambs frisking in meadows found only in Paradise? A thing or a person, who was accounted a thing by business, had to have cash value; otherwise, it was trash. The future — I'd have visions of it, though I couldn't levitate like Daniel Dunglas Home — reeks of sentimentality, which papers over everything, no matter how dire. Maybe the nineteenth century was more honest because it made less a pretense of compassion. Entrepreneurs, financiers, industrialists, and company directors wrung money from the world, as you or I would juice an orange before tossing away the skin.

Outstanding among cutthroats were the railroad barons. Their ruthless disregard of the disenfranchised and of the land they savaged increased with every mile of track. Perhaps the granite difficulties of the enterprise hardened their hearts. The Union Pacific didn't buy the car that had borne the dead president to his rest in order to commemorate his life, but to conduct its affairs in luxury. Not a shrine or even a museum, the Lincoln car was just a piece of rolling stock, more sumptuous than the rest. In the winter of 1866, not a word of this jeremiad against the money-mongers would have crossed my mind. What did engross me was my new uniform.

Dr. Thomas Durant — he insisted on the Dr. — was vice president of the Union Pacific when I arrived in Omaha. Stock manipulator, smuggler of contraband Confederate cotton, war profiteer, and among the first to take advantage of the new limited liability incorporation laws allowing him to slip out of his financial obligations as smoothly as a duck from water — Durant earned the admiration of America's biggest crooks. In one boondoggle, he ordered that track be laid in devious oxbows, instead of straight lines, to squeeze wartime profits from the beleaguered federal government, which paid for new railroad construction by the mile. After two and a half years of weaseling, the Union Pacific had advanced only forty miles west of Omaha. Curious, how one lie can get a man jailed for being a fraud, while another can get him rich — or a Medal of Honor. In the panic of 1873, Durant would lose everything he'd managed to steal in his lifetime and spend the balance sunk in a swamp of litigation. But in the winter of '66, he was a king of the mountain, rolling rocks down on anybody wanting to dethrone him.

When the Lincoln car arrived at the South Tenth Street Depot, Durant sent for me. I washed my face, slicked down my hair, blackened my boots, and walked across the rail yard to his office. Smiling through his beard, he rose from behind a big walnut desk, as if he meant to hornswoggle me into putting money into one of his concerns. I thought he must have confused me with some other army sergeant; I was still wearing my uniform, which had been, admittedly, growing shabby. But no, he knew me as soon as I stepped through the door.

"Stephen Moran," he said, extending a fleshy hand like a prince of the church so that I wondered if I ought to kiss his signet ring. Instead, I stiffened to attention, as was my habit in the presence of lordly beings like generals, aldermen, and cops. Even ruffians appreciate the oil of servility's usefulness in situations where wriggling and weaseling are called for. "Sit down and make yourself comfortable."

I sat in an overstuffed chair. He opened a humidor and offered me a Honduran cigar.

"Thank you, sir," I said, accepting the cigar and sniffing its length appreciatively. It smelled deliciously of cedar and vanilla. I was about to bite off its end, when he handed me a little silver scissors made for the beheading of expensive stogies.

"You'll need to learn how to behave among gentlemen," he said, leaning back in his swivel chair and eyeing the sooted ceiling.

I flushed with egotistical satisfaction and wished the girl could see me hobnobbing with a railroad millionaire, until I remembered I'd sworn to put her out of my mind forever. Durant's chair squawked as he broke off his contemplation of the ceiling, planted his elbows on the desk, and looked me in the eye. (That particular expression was tailor-made for a man with only one of them.)

"Stephen, you've got friends in high places," he said shrewdly.

The most elevated person I could — at a stretch — claim as a friend was a Tammany Hall alderman locked up for graft. I thought the wisest course was to say nothing and let Durant tip his hand.

"I received a telegram from my good friend President Johnson." He paused a moment to calculate the effect of his name-dropping. I put on an awestruck face, which gratified him. He was one of those men who needed the adulation even of a no-account like me. I saw no harm in it and amplified my awe with a whistle, such as one gives to signify an envious astonishment. Andrew Johnson's origins may have been humble (his mother had been a laundress), but he was no Lincoln. His meteoric rise was the result of an assassin's bullet to the far greater man. Like Durant, Johnson would become famous for his crookedness. But the history of the age had yet to be written, and a boy might well be impressed by a sharpster in a fancy cravat. "President Johnson asked me to take you under my wing as a special favor to General Grant. I believe you're acquainted with the general?"

"I am, sir. He gave me this."

I pointed to my medal as proudly as if I'd earned it.

"So I've been led to understand."

He nodded and, leaning across the desk, fingered the decoration's engraving. A morbidly curious man might have done likewise to a goiter.

I couldn't imagine how Grant had learned of my expulsion from Illinois unless he'd read about it in the papers. But why he should have concerned himself with me remains an enduring mystery. The belief I'd entertained once or twice before — that I might have a destiny, that I was intended for a place at the table among the grown-ups — once more took hold. Durant had something else in mind, however; I wasn't to sit at the table, but to wait on it.

"I'm offering you the job of steward aboard the Lincoln parlor car, although we won't be referring to it as such. I'm having it renovated as a private carriage. Your job will be to make certain our directors and guests are comfortable. When the car is idle, you'll spruce it up. I'll find you other things to do, as well. There's no end of work to be done at a rail yard. You will enjoy learning about the railroad business, Stephen. It's fascinating, I assure you. Do you accept?"

I accepted, pretending to be pleased. What else could I have done? Omaha in January is a bitterly cold place to be stranded without money. The moon must be like this, I had thought, walking to Durant's shed over snow peppered with cinders: its cold dust and bitter loneliness.

"Fine! Of course, you can't wear your old uniform. Besides, as I understand it, you're no longer in the army. After you leave here, present yourself at the quartermaster's depot and have them run you up a smart white serge jacket and trousers. You can wear your medal; it'll show what caliber of man the Union Pacific employs."

I nearly blushed to have heard myself called a man. I was small, skinny, and looked young for my years. My eye patch and the skeptical cast to my surviving orb did nothing to confute the impression of a general youthfulness.

His eyes wandered off to a memorandum on his desk as he suddenly lost interest in me. I stood and saluted him; I could not have saluted the general himself more correctly, though I'd taken a dislike to Dr. Thomas Durant — not for his moral failings, which I knew nothing about. I might have liked him better had I known he was a thief. What I couldn't abide was insincerity (except my own). Durant's benevolence covered his like the veneer on a piano. You'd never know how false he was until you played him. He might have fooled an ordinary boy of seventeen, but not me. I had sucked on the tit of disillusionment and teethed on the bitter root of cynicism. I was on my way to the misanthropy that would sour me. You know that I grew into something better, but I still had one more man to kill before I stumbled on goodness. Not such as brimstone sniffers praise, but what is sometimes found in men (and in women, too) on the frontiers of experience and hard living.

I went to the depot and got myself outfitted as a steward so that I could get through the winter without starving or freezing to death. I remained one until I was twenty-two. Durant never again spoke to me as if I were a special case, and when he referred to my Medal of Honor at all, it was scornfully, as though he'd looked into my heart and seen there just another fraud.

I'd never known any Chinese, though I'd seen them in the Devil's Arcade, mincing down the sidewalk, their pigtails swinging. They worked as cigar rollers and cobblers, mostly. I never gave them much thought, except to yell a wisecrack their way when I was feeling mean. There weren't many in Omaha at the time, but plenty were breaking their backs for the Central Pacific. They led a sorry life no white man would have tolerated. They'd fled civil war and the Heavenly Kingdom of Great Peace, where they hadn't stood a Chinaman's chance, to search for Gum Sham in California: the fabulous Mountain of Gold. Finding hunger and cruelty, tens of thousands of Chinese went to work building the transcontinental railroad, which was progressing like a wool scarf knitted and purled by a blind old woman with rheumatism. The "Celestials" — the insult *chink* hadn't yet been coined — were given the worst jobs like, wagon-loading, ballasting, or dynamiting the far

West's flinty terrain: a "ruinous space," a Boston paper called it. Their industry earned them a lower wage than the Irish; their death, a place for their bones in a wagon car destined for Sacramento. Jack Casement, the Union Pacific's man in charge of construction, admired the "cone hats" because they weren't fractious, fussy, scared of "firecrackers," or liable to strike for better wages. Besides, their ancestors had built "the world's biggest piece of masonry."

Yellow men can go bad the same as white men. How could it be otherwise, given the universal temptation to bite the outlawed apple? But a story is a kind of sieve, and I've let the Chinese workers sift out extra fine; the Irish, I've made the chaff. It isn't fair, but being a Mick myself, I feel entitled to the prejudice. Life is truly rendered in subtle tones — to speak like a photographer — but its drama is made more powerful by the stark contrast of chiaroscuro. Every storyteller knows as much.

Chen Shi was pedaling like mad on a Singer machine, illuminated by a rain-spattered skylight at the back of the depot, surrounded by bolts of cloth, lint, rubbish, and nests of threads. I watched him push a length of serge this way and that under the flying needle. After a while, he peered up at me through wire-rim spectacles; his eyes were dull and watery.

"You want me make something nice?" he asked.

I must've smirked to hear him speak. His English was broken; the words sounded like a mangle had wrung them of articulation. Later on, I gave a damned fine impersonation of Chen to a track foreman. He was a Methodist from Arkansas, who could, I thought, be counted on to share in my scorn for an inferior race. He flabbergasted me by asking if I could speak Mandarin. As if I'd want to! I found out later that his sister belonged to a missionary society on the Yellow River.

"Dr. Durant has made me his personal steward aboard the Lincoln parlor car," I said with the self-importance of a little man serving a writ. While I was not so inclined as formerly to put on airs, I could still lord it over a Chinaman.

To give Chen's ears every opportunity to take in my meaning, I pronounced each word distinctly and strikingly, as if I were stamping Lady Liberty on a half-cent piece. He was not in the least impressed. Next, I pointed to my sergeant's stripes and my Medal of Honor. He stared at them blankly.

The man's a fool, I said to myself. Without a word, he got up from his machine and measured me with a cloth tape. His fingers were long and delicate, like a piano player's or a cardsharp's yellowed by cigarettes.

"Not today," he said. "You come next day."

God Almighty, what a hash! But my new uniform fit me to perfection. Admiring myself in a cheval glass next to Chen's machine, I must've been preening like a girl — so taken was I by my reflection. I was used to seeing myself in worn-out blue coat and pants, when I bothered to look at all. I turned this way and that and twisted my head to see my back. Chen laughed at me! My neck grew warm with embarrassment. I wheeled on the yellow bastard and would have gone for him if something in his eyes hadn't stopped me. What I saw was a look of amusement, such as you'd see on the face of a white man who'd just seen someone make himself ridiculous.

"How do I look?" I asked in a tone of voice that slid from defiance to self-mockery, like a slide whistle in a vaudeville show or a trombone braying a circus "screamer."

"A bottle of milk," he replied with a frankness different from what I'd have expected from a devious Asiatic.

Chen and I got on well together, although I never felt so close to him as I would have if he'd been white. I'm sure he wished I were one of his own kind. After waiting on the "beaver hats" visiting a godforsaken railhead, I would go to the quartermaster's to see him. Except as the company tailor, he seldom had contact with the other Caucasians. When he did, he spoke "chop-chop," so as not to provoke them. His English was almost as good as mine, since he'd learned it at a mission school in China. I'd have thought him cowardly if not for a scar on his cheek, put there by a teamster's whip when Chen refused to be driven from the street into a muddy slough.

Chen shared a room near the packinghouse with four other Chinese. Two didn't speak his dialect. He must have been lonely. Once, he invited me home (we'll call it that, regardless of its meager comforts) to eat with him. According to his lights, to share a meal with a man was to honor him. The room was wretched, dark, and crowded, but I was unfazed, having grown up in squalor. The noise of five Chinamen squabbling while they chopped vegetables reminded me of the tenement — and a yard full of outraged turkeys. Having finished our meal (a peculiar sort of stew I didn't much care for), we sat and smoked — the last of the general's cigars for me, a long pipe like a Dutchman's for Chen.

"My mother and father," he said, showing me a tintype portrait of a severe man wearing a quilted jacket and a skullcap and a woman staring pensively. Her eyes seemed to be asking something of me. I think I must have shivered with the uncanniness of her gaze. Chen nodded sympathetically through a cloud of tobacco smoke; perhaps her eyes penetrated him, also, each time he looked at the picture. "You seem surprised," he said, tactfully finding a subject other than what his mother's gaze might mean.

"I didn't think Chinamen had heard of cameras," I said, happy that the conversation had veered. I had no wish to speculate on what pain a Chinese woman might feel, its causes and intensity. I didn't understand women of my own kind, much less those that had their feet bound.

He laughed, and I was reassured to hear a laugh like anybody else's. We're not the same, I thought, but we're not unknowable or untranslatable.

In 1866, the Chinese were more mysterious to most Americans than Negroes, Indians, or Jews, for whom the rituals of torment had been worked out long before. It takes time to perfect cruelty — to coin terms of abuse with which to belittle and defame. We had to learn to intone *nigger, redskin, hymie, chink, dago, greaser,* et cetera, before we could turn individual meanness into a national spite. It galled me to hear myself called a "papist Mick" and a "mackerel snapper," but I couldn't bloody the mouths of the whole hidebound host bent on degrading me — no, not even if I'd been the rough-and-tumble sort. Poor bastards like Chen get to know the taste of dirt long before they lie down in it to take their eternal rest.

I remember how I'd hated the old black man at the feed and grain store. I'd wanted to choke the life out of him. I'd wanted to scream that I had lost my eye for the sole purpose of freeing him and his descendants. And Spotswood — what had I really thought of him? To this day, I do not understand rage's (or is it envy's or merely fear's?) heat, which can twist a man from his true self, like an iron rod denatured in the forge.

The Hundredth Meridian, Nebraska Territory, October 20, 1866

At the hundredth meridian, I met a woman who must not have read Paul's Letter to the

Ephesians concerning submission and obedience: She bent for nobody and did what she pleased. A train had been made up to carry dignitaries, newspaper writers, and eastern moneymen to the Union Pacific's latest railhead, two hundred and fifty miles west of Omaha. Durant and his gang, installed like sultans aboard the old Lincoln car, rode west with a haughty, high-toned chef from Frisco to fry their steaks and me to serve the whiskey. After nearly a year's swanning up and down the line in my white suit, I had learned how to glare critically at the silverware, polish the crystal glasses, dust the shoulders of the bottles, and dance in attendance, like a monkey on a stick. I was a self-satisfied mug whose throat would have been cut in the Five Points just to put my nose out of joint. What else could you expect of someone who finds himself by divine accident in the midst of fabulous wealth and power? I didn't fall into temptation so much as hurl myself at it. It was my Gilded Age, however brief.

While the barons made speeches, heard their vision and industry praised by a pack of bootlickers, and postured for the photographers, heads behind drapes to immortalize this great milestone on the way to Utah, I ogled a redhead in boots and a lumberman's coat buttoned over a blue satin dress. I remember her name! Kari Lund. She and her father operated a traveling store in a prairie wagon they'd driven from St. Louis. They rattled up and down the lengthening track, selling whiskey, tobacco, corned beef, potatoes, and sundries. Old man Lund could also barber and shave a man, if any required tonsorial attention. But the Irish were not overly fastidious out of doors, and the coolies, who liked to be clean and tidy, were forbidden to cut their pigtails on pain of death, should they ever return shorn to China. Foreigners have their ways; we have ours.

Kari was not impressed by my milk white uniform or my Medal of Honor. I don't think she thought much of me. She was a head taller, and her body outside of her clothes had a rude good health mine never did. Maybe she liked my face. Maybe she was bored. In any case, she let me have her in what passed for a bedroom inside the wagon while Papa Elof was away with the horses, replenishing the stock. It cannot be said that I "took her"; she'd have broken my nose for me had I tried. The experience surpassed my clumsy initiation in the chaplains' crib and the sad wreck I'd made of desire in Chicago. Love would always be an ordeal, although I would look for it, like everyone else. Maybe I'd kept company with death too long during that twelve-day journey to the grave to find it. Despite her grit, Kari was gentle while we grappled and cleaved. She might have seen herself a missionary, bringing the comforts of her ample body to men lost and baffled by yearning on the vast plains. Most men are no better than godforsaken heathens.

When the quilt slipped from her breasts, I was startled by their soft, round fullness, so unfamiliar in that harsh country. Our skins blushed in the wavering light from the stove. The heat was luxurious. I felt a motion in my arms and legs as a river must when its ice begins to thaw. I exulted in the moment, however unreal. I knew enough of life to realize its brevity and the transience of both its pains and pleasures. We lay there while night sealed the prairie with a chill silence, its stars obedient to an ancient rule, their commotion heard only by dogs howling in the midst of a godless solitude. In their private car, warmed by brandy and cigars, Durant's gang plotted to carve up the emptiness to their own advantage. So I imagined. From what I knew of their kind, my guess was a good one.

Greed is not exclusive to empire builders

like Durant, who believed it a necessary vice if civilization was to take root and thrive. After Mr. Lincoln was murdered, Ford's Theatre was stripped of its seats by profiteers whose ambition did not encompass territories, but only what could be carted off in a wagon or two. I suppose, in my own modest way, I was ambitious for a larger life. I was enamored of myself each time I put on that ridiculous white uniform. I enjoyed rich men's company. I must have flattered myself a kind of soldier sent into the land of plenty to steal as much as he could carry, like one of Sherman's "bummers" during his ardent march to the sea. I filched their cigars, liquor, tinned meat, buffalo tongue, and oysters. Being among them as they crossed their immense kingdom, surrounded by money and luxury, I must have believed something of theirs would rub off. I'm almost sure that is how it was for me. I fancied myself an up-and-comer. Afterward, when I was no longer a steward and was once more surrounded by ordinary men, I lost my self-importance. I do owe my rich and powerful patron one thing, however: my infatuation with photography, which commenced on that cold October morning on the hundredth meridian.

Three shrill blasts of the locomotive's whistle woke Kari and me, the wild dogs in their holes, and the pig in its mire beside the wagon. We dressed and went outside while the eastern stars were giving way to the lightening sky. A photographer had set up his camera to capture the train's departure on a wet-glass plate. During the ceremony, my mind had been elsewhere, but as he handled the maple box and its brass cylinder, my interest grew. I asked how it worked; he mumbled a gruff reply from under the curtain. He was too preoccupied, or hungover, or the day far too early to satisfy my curiosity.

Kari insisted he take our picture. He withdrew his head from behind the curtain and — liking the look of her, I guess — agreed. I kept it with me until I lost my wallet at the Little Bighorn. She stood upright and stiff, as was the custom for portraits of the time. You couldn't tell her hair was red, of course. But her face managed to relax during the exposure. She almost smiled. In the last instant before the photographer covered the lens, I turned my head, wanting to see her handsome profile, her slightly parted lips revealing a tooth. In the picture, my face was blurred. Durant and his chums were waiting on the car's rear platform, where I had stood, often at night, with Jericho to play taps for a man whom I'd never heard speak. There was no time to take a second photograph of a lovesick boy.

I don't recall what Kari and I said to each other. Nothing of consequence. Until now, I haven't been a man to unburden himself. What lay deep stayed deep. I was with her for a brief time, is all, like Odysseus in the arms of Circe, forgetting his way home. Only I had none. Lovesick! I was always ready to give my heart, yet I would never have given it entirely. Something in me wanted to keep itself secret and apart. Unless at my core, there was nothing to give.

Feeling Kari's heat when we lay together, I recalled the winter nights when my mother had taken me into bed beside her to stop me from shivering. She was thin and had little heat to spare. I was glad she hadn't died of consumption: I would have blamed myself for stealing her vitality, as a cat is said to steal a baby's breath. She always feared a Brooklyn pauper's grave.

"I want to be buried in the cemetery at Dún Laoghaire," she used to say.

She ended among the destitute on Ward's Island. Did these morbid thoughts turn on my mind's lathe during the night in Kari's wagon, or is the recollection of that night darkened now by what I found on my return to Omaha?

"Did you enjoy the lady?" Reynolds asked while I poured him his favorite whiskey.

He was one of the moneybags, for whom I had a special loathing. He leered sufficiently to make me almost forget myself. His mockery twisted suddenly into a challenge. He fixed me with his coldest stare and waited for my reply.

"I did, sir."

"You'll forgive me, I'm sure, if I insist on hearing the details of your conquest. When old men lose their juice, their curiosity becomes inflamed."

He tossed the drink down his gullet, like kerosene meant to fuel the flames of a lurid imagination. In time, I would learn to understand men like him. I met enough of his kind, and their fantasies did not always concern sexual intercourse. There were others nostalgic for their robust past: for a strong body or a mind delighting in the subjugation — by fear or humiliation — of Indians, blacks, Chinese, coyotes, bison, women. Often it doesn't matter what, so long as prejudice has an object. Some men (some women, also, to insist on equality) are impelled to cultivate the seeds of enmity — sown how, why, or by whom, it little matters. George Armstrong Custer, for instance.

I first met him in '74, on the Black Hills Expedition. I photographed his conquests, his triumphs, his acquisitions. I remember how, after he had killed a bear, his eyes underneath the yellow curls looked glazed and far away, like those of a man who'd just rolled off a woman's belly. In the varnished negative, his face was gruesome, as it might have been were light to fall on it suddenly in a tomb. It is always so to see the normal tones reversed, but in Custer's case, the effect was striking. At least, my imagination — yeasty after a disastrous winter with the Ute — found it so. Let's say that the photograph had unmasked a man intended for an unusual destiny — an inhuman one, because it had nothing to do with ordinary men. I couldn't foresee the Little Bighorn — I hadn't yet met Crazy Horse — but I saw in Custer's face the smirk of a man whose name would be writ large in our history. In that he seemed to venerate killing like a holy office, I supposed his contribution would be infamous. He had ambition, the good opinion of his superiors, and a regiment at his disposal. Otherwise, Custer was no different from a man who — his snoot full of cheap rye on a Saturday night — drags his wife by the hair around the kitchen, beats his children, kicks his dog, or wages war against a hill of ants. So perhaps Custer's destiny was not an inhuman one after all.

I knew a man in Santa Fe, who took offense at a horde of ants in the ground behind his house. They got on his nerves, he said; they troubled his dreams and disturbed his rest. In time, they interfered with his work and threatened his livelihood. Not that they ever came inside the house — that wasn't it. His hatred, which swelled into a fury, was unreasoning; it had no practical point or issue. He would stomp on them as they filed in and out of the hole to their nest: a black string that he made, in his madness, into a fetish. He lay awake at night, hearing them scurry on the hard earth, plotting their extermination, rejoicing in its contemplation. But the ants were indifferent to his stratagems. Unable to destroy their race by killing them singly, he blocked the entrance, flattened the hill with a shovel, dug up the nest. But always the ants found their way out again — the tribe apparently numberless. Finally, he soaked the ground with kerosene. The fire meant to be the ants' holocaust burned down his house. The ants endured. A pretty fable.

I shouldn't have appeased Reynolds's appetite. I ought to have spat in his eye, taken off my idiotic uniform, and reentered the world. Had I ever been in it? But those were hard times, and I was in the wilderness. It was no golden age after all, not for upstarts who might suddenly decide they could mouth off to their betters. The Declaration of Independence was not for people like me. Poverty had not been abolished, or cruelty outlawed, or greed shamed into nonexistence. Life on the frontier was harassed by savages, plagued by sickness, made miserable by hunger and cold. Out on my own, I could expect to live considerably fewer than three score years and ten. Not being Thoreau, Emerson, John Brown, Frederick Douglas, Clara Barton, Lincoln, or Frederick Aiken, I behaved in keeping with my character and age. I told Reynolds what he wanted to know. I stoked his inferno and saw how his eyes sparked, then glazed over, like a priest's vouchsafed a glimpse of Paradise.

Omaha, Nebraska Territory, October 24, 1866–December 4, 1866

Where the tailors worked, a German was pedaling the Singer. I wanted to tell Chen about my night inside the wagon in the middle of nowhere, how in the morning the gray plain sprawled to the encircling horizon, and about the photographer who'd fixed — he said "forever" — the light from a Swedish woman on a pane of glass. It never occurred to me to call Chen my friend; I hadn't the habit or knack of friendship. There isn't the sentimental strain in me you sometimes find in men whose childhood was grim. They see themselves like an urchin in a Dickens novel: a bleak heart sweetened by suffering. They look back fondly on their mistreated youthful selves. My childhood was brief and is best forgotten.

"Where's Chen?" I asked the German, his head bent low over his work. In the noise of the machine — a brittle *rattattat* like a Gatling gun — he hadn't heard me. I asked again, this time shouting, "Where is Chen?"

He stopped his pedaling, let the cloth rest, and raised his bleary eyes to me. He was older than Chen and looked worn, frayed, and wrinkled.

"Dead," he replied grudgingly, annoyed by the interruption. He was paid by the piece — and what did it matter to him that the railroad had lost a Chinaman? The coolie army had grown to thirteen thousand blue-jacketed men as the tracks leaped toward Utah, in advance of the fire-breathing dragons of the New World.

"How?" I asked. He gave me an infuriating sauerkraut smirk that made me want to brain him. "What happened to him?"

"He got a pain in his stomach, vomited, and died," said the German brusquely, turning back to his work.

I knew I'd have to put a stick of dynamite up this stiff-backed Prussian's ass to make him talkative. I left him to his sewing and went to find the depot quartermaster.

"He died of the 'trembles,' " he said, with a shrug that consigned Chen to the hell reserved for heathens and infidels. You've heard of it, I'm sure, Jay. It comes from drinking milk from a cow that's grazed on white snakeroot.

He was in the middle of counting shovels and had no time for "Durant's Puppy," as I was known — with good reason, I suppose. The Irish called me "Durant's Nigger." They'd have had my liver on toast ever since General Jack had ordered me to blow reveille at five o'clock on any Monday morning I happened to be in Omaha. They would wake with thick tongues and big heads after a half day's rest, which meant, for most, a booze-up in the Irish saloon. General Jack never missed an opportunity to needle the "worthless bog trotters" for proving themselves even lower than his yellow drudges.

That night, I went to see the men who'd shared Chen's room.

"What happen Chen?" I asked in pidgin English. They stood like a quartet of Easter Island statues, poker-faced and inscrutable. I tried shouting next, as if their incomprehension were the result of ear wax. "What happen Chen?" They must have been used to bellowing white men, for they never even flinched. Frustrated, I impersonated someone with the shakes and a bellyache. The charade must have appeared comical to the Chinamen. They jabbered among themselves critically, and then one whose ear was a scorched stump laughed. Irked, I knocked him down. He was smaller than I, and I gloated to see his surprise. I left the room, haughty as a general delivering an ultimatum to a beaten foe. I was sorry for it later — that, and much else besides.

Passing the cattle pens on the walk back to the depot, I suddenly recalled a conversation I'd had with Chen.

"Are there cows in China?" I'd asked, betraying once more my ignorance of the wider world.

He smiled tolerantly. "Yes, but we do not

drink so much milk as you. I never do; it disagrees with me."

In the morning, I went to the infirmary to talk to the company doctor.

"I want to ask you about Chen Shi," I said.

"Who is Chen Shi?"

"The Chinese tailor who died of the trembles."

"Go on," he said, hooking his ankles around the legs of the stool. The black hairs on his legs poked through his checkered socks.

"Chen didn't drink milk," I told him. "It didn't agree with him."

"There're a hundred ways to die," he said, with a shrug that looked like helplessness. He glanced at a sickbed where a man was pledged to one of them. "He could've been bitten by a rattler. Or maybe someone put white snakeroot or arsenic in his tea. He was Chinese; he was bound to have enemies."

Like a German tailor, I thought. Or the quartermaster, also German. History will show you can't trust a stinking sauerkraut.

The infirmary smelled like the Armory Square Hospital, where my fiction had been hatched, and I was itching to leave. There was nothing I could do for Chen. I wasn't about to demand an inquest or to pursue the poisoner. I'm no Auguste Dupin.

"Do you know where Chen's buried?" I asked the doctor, who had unhooked his ankles from the stool and was listening to the dying man's chest with a stethoscope. I considered the instrument superfluous. I could hear the croup and rattle of pneumonia from across the room.

"In the 'Chinese cemetery' behind the train shed. Look for fresh-turned earth."

I took Jericho, determined to play taps over Chen's grave. I could be a vain and pompous ass in those days. There were only a few graves; most of the Chinese workers died in California and Nevada, dynamiting through the Sierras — blown to bits or buried beneath tons of American rock. A sad ending for those who'd dreamed, once, of gold ingots. Each grave had a cross for decoration. Was it ignorance or malice to have buried them like Methodists? Or did a high-minded evangelist with a shovel intend to convert the misbegotten heathen when they could no longer object? I knelt — it might've been the first time in history that a white man had knelt before a Chinaman, quick or dead. Not knowing any Chinese prayers, I said a Catholic grace: "We give Thee thanks, Almighty God, for all Thy benefits, and for the poor souls of the faithful departed; through the mercy of God, may they rest in peace. Amen." I crossed myself, and then I blew taps. I couldn't have done better if it were Abraham Lincoln himself lying in the ground before me. I was so moved that tears started up in my eye. Seized by a fit of generosity, I took off my medal and laid it at the foot of the cross. I brushed the loose dirt from my white-capped knees and left the corpses to go about their ghastly business. I hadn't walked fifty yards when I changed my mind and went back for my medal. Who knew? I might need it yet.

I never found a man of any race to replace Chen — excepting you. You've been decent and a friend. On Sunday afternoons, Chen and I would walk the length and breadth of Omaha, although, in 1866, there was nothing about it you'd call picturesque. Omaha was a machine for slaughtering, packing, and shipping cattle. For all its monotony and stink, the town had its share of amusements — drinking holes and whorehouses, naturally, but I'd have been embarrassed to be seen in either place with Chen. What I mean is, I'd have been ashamed of myself. He had more of a civilizing effect on me than all the high-and-mighty, holier-than-thou con men I'd known in my wanderings.

China has an ancient civilization. It was bound to have seeped into Chen at birth and to have changed me a little during the time I was steeped in him, so to speak.

He tended to spice his remarks with epigrams. One I remember was "Stars that outshine the rest are the first to disappear." I don't know if it was Confucius's saying or Chen's own. Product of a self-effacing race, he disapproved of my inclination to show off, which he attributed to shallowness and insecurity. I was hardly more than a boy! He thought it a dangerous folly to wear a snow-white uniform in a wilderness peopled by the Irish and the Indians. Chen's gift was to fit himself to circumstances. I'd advocate it, if his life hadn't been cut short.

With nothing to do anymore in my idle hours, I undertook my education. I wish I could tell you that I had Chen's example in mind. But the truth is, I became an avid reader by chance. I was searching the depot warehouse for a case of scotch that Durant had ordered from New York, when I found a crate of books intended, by some eastern philanthropic society, for Omaha's circulating library. A library, circulating or otherwise, had not yet been thought of for a town consisting mostly of illiterate Irishmen, foreigners, and cowboys herding steers into cattle pens by waving their Boss of the Plains hats and making their own version of Whitman's "barbaric yawp." I gave a coolie two bits to haul the crate to the tool car hitched behind Durant's traveling boardroom, where I had my quarters; and in the long evenings when I wasn't licking boots and kissing backsides, I read. In the three and a half years remaining to me as Durant's Puppy, I read *The Scarlet Letter, Silas Marner, The Autobiography of Benjamin Franklin, Pride and Prejudice, Gulliver's Travels, The Marble Faun, Moby-Dick, Knickerbocker's History of New York, The Red Rover, David Copperfield, Uncle Tom's Cabin, The Woman in White, Adam Bede, The Age of Fable, Bleak House,* illustrated by Phiz, *The Origin of Species,* which could have found its way into the crate only by chance or spitefulness, and *The Diary of a Superfluous Man,* whose title spoke to the situation of a boy no more central to the great events in which he found himself than a gnat in the halls of Congress. I had fallen in my own estimation since leaving the army, but I'd be sitting in the catbird seat once again.

With no formal education and little experience in reading (beyond Durant's private papers, which I would pull from his briefcase and peruse), I could never have wormed my way through all those books if it hadn't been for Patrick Landy. He'd been sent by an eastern newspaper to write an article deploring the Johnson administration's neglect of the Lincoln parlor car: a "national disgrace" and "the final quietus to the man who saved the Union." I met Landy the month following Chen's murder (for so I swear it to have been), when he visited the Union Pacific shed. One of my duties was to scare off trespassers and vandals. Personally, I did not think my face or manner could scare a boy on his way to a Baptist picnic. But the car had been "egged" once already by die-hard secessionists, and Durant insisted I keep watch. This was his price for letting me stay in a corner of the tool car — dirty with pigeon droppings and grease. When I suggested he furnish me with a firearm, he replied fleeringly that my bugle would be enough to intimidate any mischief makers and, if I were overrun, to signal for help. So I met Landy for the first time with Jericho at the ready.

"I'm not partial to bugle music," he said disarmingly when I had answered his knock on the old parlor car's back door.

"What do you want?" I asked with as convincing a show of grit as I could muster.

I couldn't have been more surprised by the burly man's abrupt appearance if he'd been a grampus heaved up on my doorstep by the night tide.

By now you know I was never brave — not as a boy, not as a man. I'm not saying I ran from trouble (at least not always), but I would feel something inside my nerves and gut give way at trouble's approach, making my gorge rise, as well as the little hairs on my neck. Antagonism did not come naturally to me, unless the other party to the conflict happened to be a smaller man. Landy must've seen my apprehension in the way I shuffled and fidgeted with Jericho, but he had tact enough not to belittle me.

"I'm a reporter for the *Chicago Daily Tribune,*" he said in a peaceable voice belied by his robust presence. "Mind if I take a look around?"

I didn't see any reason to bar entrance to a gentleman of the press or to blow Jericho for reinforcements, so I opened the door wide and let him come in. Reading by the light of a single candle set on the table, I hadn't noticed when the shadows engulfed the narrow car. I lit the wall sconces, and their reflected light bloomed suddenly, gilding each windowpane. Mr. Lincoln's funeral coach still retained its opulence; the varnished wood of the coffered panels and carved furniture gleamed, the crystal shone, and the tapestried chairs and sofas caught glints of light in their shiny threads.

"People back east think it's a shame the car that bore Abe Lincoln to his tomb ended up a pleasure coach for rich men," he said, putting his hat on the table in a disdainful way that would prove his worth to these same men had they been there to see it. "Lincoln was a man of the people, and his parlor car rightfully belongs to the people. I was sent out here to write a piece about the car's employment by a gang of plutocrats who don't give a damn for sentiment or democracy." He held his horses a moment, studying a bottle of Jameson Irish whiskey, like an ornithologist beholding an exotic bird landed on a steaming pile of Barren Island "putrescibles." Conscientiousness carried the day over liquid temptation — imported, you would have thought, expressly for his ruin. "You're an Irish lad, by the look of you."

"I am," I said.

"What does your mother call you?" he asked, shunting down a spur from the main track of his thought, like a locomotive when the points are changed.

"She *called* me Stephen. She's dead."

I was reclining on a horsehair sofa in order to prove my own equality and democratic pluck. Besides, I was not obliged to wait on newspapermen without an appointment.

"My condolences. A Dublin girl, was she, during her days in God's second Eden? I'm not one of those traitors who call Ireland His most fantastic mistake. They were whelped by an angry god."

"Dún Laoghaire."

"I'm pleased to hear you call it by its given name instead of Kingstown. Goddamn the British Empire!" His gaze shifted again to the bottle in token of his patriotism, but he quickly broke its spellbinding thread with a shake of his heavy jowls, broken-veined by drink, as if to disabuse himself of a mirage. "What are you reading?"

"*Silas Marner.*"

"There's a tale of penny-pinching greed Durant and his fellow robber barons should be forced to eat raw and uncooked!" he bawled.

Here now, I thought, is the true timbre of the big blustering Mick. I admit I found his performance entertaining and, hoping for more, baited him.

"You should see the steaks and oysters they throw down their gullets," I said. "Chased with the best whiskey."

I recalled the hard bread, salt, and coffee we had eaten in the field and wished that Durant and his cronies would choke on their luxuries. The wish, no more than a spark, cooled, and the comedy continued.

"I wouldn't mind a drop."

"Sure thing, Mr. Landy!" I said, jumping up to fetch General Jack's bottle of Irish.

"There's nothing like the sound of good whiskey falling lightly in a glass," he remarked appreciatively when I poured him out a double jigger's worth. He smacked his lips, raised his glass, and saluted me with the ceremony of Grant doffing his hat to Lee at Appomattox Court House. "May you be in heaven a full half hour before the devil knows you're dead."

He drank it off, and I stood poised to pour him another. But he turned his shot glass upside down.

"Thank you, but I don't want to forget the reason why I've come."

This is no ordinary Irishman, I said to myself, marveling at his restraint in the presence of Dublin's most celebrated mash. He composed himself, cleared his throat rhetorically, and then asked to hear me recite my history. Except for how I'd lost my eye to my own carelessness, I told him the truth. I don't know why I was mostly honest with him, unless his repugnance for crooks and fakes encouraged me to be factual. As I told my tale — it took me some time to gather the threads and, frequently having dropped them in befuddlement, pick them up again — Landy would nod, his spectacles flashing with candlelight a semaphore of compassion or indignation, appropriate to each pitiful incident.

"And did you know Mr. Lincoln?" he asked when I'd finished talking.

"I knew him dead," I said, "better than anyone else, including his wife, who was prostrate in Washington during the twelve days it took to take him home. I kept him company during the long, silent nights the train traveled between wakes. I'd sit in this car, with only the candles on the two coffins to shoulder the darkness, and I'd think all the grand and terrible thoughts that go through the mind of a person contemplating a corpse. I had two corpses to ponder: one short, the other extra long."

"It would have scared the bejesus out of most!" Landy said, his whistle wet with remnant booze his shockingly pink tongue had leached from his mustache.

I was pleased with the courage I'd shown, though I hadn't recognized it until now.

"I met Walt Whitman," I said. "The poet."

"A scurrilous man! He violates the conventions of metrical poetry and decency."

Ignorant of poetry, I felt it prudent to change the subject.

"And General Grant. He gave me this."

I showed him the medal.

"If I can fit you into my article, I will," he said. "What's the last name?"

"Moran."

He wrote down my name in his notebook, or pretended to. "Stephen Moran," he said grandly, composing with his index finger a headline in the air: THE BUGLE BOY & HIS LONELY VIGIL.

I never saw my name or story in the *Chicago Daily Tribune.* But Landy was instrumental in my education. The paper kept him in Omaha to report on the railroad's westward progress. In the evenings when I was in town, I'd sit and read in a corner of his office. He'd help me over the words I didn't know and through the tangle of thoughts I could not, at first, pick apart into sense.

The crusade to save the Lincoln funeral car failed, naturally. The railroad continued to use it to supervise construction. I lost track of it after I left the Union Pacific in 1870 to traipse across the Wasatch with my camera. I have it on good authority that it ended its days a curiosity in Minneapolis, until a prairie fire reduced it to a burned-out wreck.

Life went on, as it must till the last breath escapes us and mingles, according to the laws of natural science, with the ether. Whether it will transpire, at time's finale, into the bosom of Abraham, who showed a willingness to slaughter his son, none can say. And Abraham Lincoln? Many say he ought to have been more careful of *his* sons, who went to the killing fields by their tens and hundreds of thousands. In my opinion, Lincoln was a good man. If a man can be good. What is a good man if not one who does not believe in himself to the exclusion of others? I saw his face, remember. Not even the mortuary art could erase it entirely of gnawing doubt. Beneath the artful rouge and chalk, I saw the marks left by the demons — his countrymen's and his own — wrestled unto death. (I wish I could have photographed that face!) He was asked to bear what cannot be borne — what should not be borne. I hope never to be so tested, for I have it on the best authority that I will not bear it.

Promontory Summit, Utah Territory, May 10, 1869

On the tenth of May, in 1869, the final track was laid and the last spikes hammered home — one gold, one silver, one an alloy of gold, silver, and iron — to celebrate the "wedding of the rails": the meeting of the Union Pacific and the Central Pacific railroads, nearly a mile above sea level, at Promontory Summit, north of the Great Salt Lake. There's nary a Chinaman to be seen in A. J. Russell's famous photograph, although the final ten-mile stretch of track had been laid by a special crew of cone-hatted, blue-jacketed coolies, famous for their speed. Soon a person could travel by train from the Missouri River to Sacramento and onward by paddleboat to San Francisco Bay. If, as Durant once told me, the transcontinental railroad would be a great artery transecting America's continental empire, then the tainted blood of the East could flow, unobstructed, into the healthy body of the West, carrying religion and civilization the way conquistadores brought God and syphilis to the Indians and the Mexicans. The natives, buffalo, riches, and gods of the Old West would drown in blood. On that May day, the West began its long, slow dying.

Cheats of every stripe would flood the Great Plains and California's trackless groves with Bibles, patent medicines, whiskey, writs, moral tracts, and guns. As if the Almighty had raised the eastern seaboard from its basalt bed and tilted it, con men, cutthroats, grifters, quacks, swindlers, schemers, politicians, speculators, prospectors, profiteers, gamblers, fortune hunters, lawyers, counterfeiters, and killers tumbled west. A sour view of things, I grant you; but one borne out by the history of our age and of the age to come, when Trinity — not the Christians', but Oppenheimer's — will turn Alamogordo sand to glass. In the future, dead cities will molder behind rusting thorns no prince can ever penetrate; dirty bombs will engender tribes of lepers — not by germs, but by deadly atoms; and radioactive isotopes will be left to cool for an age or more, sealed in burial chambers with a pharaoh's curse. Instead of a photographer, I should have been a prophet, howling in a wilderness of death. I seem to know the future: It came to me in dreams. Terrible ones! Pictures, words — not exactly those, but what you might see and hear if you had eyes like an owl's and ears like a bat's. I seem to be cognizant of what's to come, Jay, without clearly understanding it. I'm like a man with his eyes closed, running his fingers over braille.

Also, on that tenth of May, I sent my medal back to Grant, now president of the United States, with a note in which I confessed the lie that had won it: "Inasmuch as I lost my eye to my own panic and carelessness, I am undeserving of the honor you bestowed on me with your own hands. Respectfully yours, Sergeant Stephen Moran, retired." I struck out "Sergeant" and wrote "Private" in its place — the only rank to which I felt myself entitled. Grant sent the medal back to me, with a brief note of his own:

THE WHITE HOUSE
WASHINGTON CITY

June 14, 1869

Dear Sergeant Moran,
If we were treated as we deserve, we'd all be in the hoosegow.

Sincerely,
U. S. Grant, President

I'd like to tell you that the occasion celebrated in the Utah high country sobered me; that it chastened me of pettiness and deceit. I'd like to think that I came to my senses in the clear air at the summit, with its austere view of distant mountains rising from an empty plateau. There is nothing like the West to solemnize a person's mood, to burn away the meanness. I would like to believe I returned my medal for some exalted reason. But looking back, I don't know why I did it. I can't say that I really know why I did anything in those days. We come to know ourselves, if we ever do at all, too late.

Part Two: Custer

I am the man, I suffered, I was there.
— Walt Whitman, *Song of Myself*

Promontory Summit, Utah Territory, May 10, 1869

While the locomotives panted for the steamy consummation of the wedding of the rails, I was looking for the true bridegrooms: the Chinese who had laid the final tracks. I had no interest in capturing the official flummery. I'd leave that to Hart, Savage, and Russell to fix expertly on their glass-plate negatives for eastern newspapers, souvenir postcards, and stereopticons. I don't know why I wanted to take the Chinamen's picture, but I suspect it had to do with Chen. On that long-gone May afternoon in Utah, I had no idea that the coolies were being feted out of sight by Jim Strowbridge in his private car. For all I knew, they might have been pitched off Promontory Summit, buried alive in one of their own excavations, or crated up for shipment to the land of their ancestors. Strowbridge was foreman for the Central Pacific, which had dug and dynamited its way from Sacramento, through the Sierra Nevada, to meet the Union Pacific near Ogden. Ever since finding out about his little soirée, I've been suspicious of the railroad's motives in whisking the Chinese crew down the line and away from the festivities.

I took a few pictures for Durant, who was my patron, of sorts. I wasn't much good yet as a photographer, and he could get all he needed from the famous cameramen in attendance. Still, I thought I'd better show him something for the railroad's money: a little legerdemain of light and shadow. The camera and darkroom setup were expensive, and "What the Lord giveth, He taketh away." If you're not sufficiently appreciative. I didn't want Durant to take back my camera. Photography had enthralled me since the day Kari and I got our portrait made at the hundredth meridian. I had what you might call an instinct for it. Edward Jackson said later that I had the makings of a first-class photographer. So I made several exposures of the two locomotives, cowcatchers kissing; of the dignitaries, chests puffed out; and of the Irish, squatting by the rails. They'd as much right to the honor as I did to my medal. Only one of the pictures turned out passably well: It showed the Union Pacific's locomotive engineer reaching toward the Central Pacific's man, holding a bottle of champagne. (You've probably seen Russell's version.)

In spite of the rough crowd packed into the picture, beneath the engineers' outstretched hands — one clutching a bottle, the other about to receive it — the photograph made me think of God in a tangle of angels, touching Adam's finger with His, although both of those gents were staunch teetotalers and probably Methodists. I'd seen an engraving of Michelangelo's famous fresco hanging in Stanton's office. It looked as out of place as a nosebleed on a wedding dress. Unless Stanton pictured himself the Lord of Hosts, adjuring shirkers with His galvanic finger. Or maybe we were meant to see Abe Lincoln in that graven image, about to give "old Mars" a vivifying jolt. War and electricity do seem to be connected by a mystic chord. Whitman wrote in *Leaves:* "I sing the Body electric,/ The armies of those I love engirth me and I engirth them . . ."

Durant had bought me the photographic

equipment in answer to my proposition. I doubt he did it to further my education or to show his appreciation for my years of servility. No, he was not that sort of man. He did nothing in his life without a mental calculation determining the advantage to himself. Durant bought me my camera because it pleased him to think of himself doing it. I knew in advance just what terms of endearment I would use to express my gratitude. Four years in service as a steward taught me the protocols by which men meet men as something other than equals. But first, I'd have to pass an unholy night with him.

The Black Hills, Wyoming Territory, August 1868

One summer's evening at a railhead in the Black Hills, Durant fell into a genial mood indicative of a profound satisfaction with the world and his privileged place in it — encouraged by whiskey and the contemplation of "his empire," sprawling in every direction beyond what the human eye could take in. He'd just returned from viewing a seven-hundred-foot wooden-truss bridge thrown across Dale Creek Gorge by his Chinese and Irish workers. Momentarily well disposed toward them, he spoke kindly to me, to whom he rarely spoke at all except to instruct me in my duties, about his past days as a surgeon in Albany, as a wheat broker, and a railroad man.

"You were acquainted with President Lincoln, I believe," he said, gazing wistfully through the carriage window at the gathering dusk.

"In a manner of speaking."

"Seeing the bridge this afternoon reminded me of another, built across the Mississippi in '56."

Pretending to be interested, I threw the bar rag, with which I'd been polishing the liquor glasses, over my shoulder and looked in his vicinity. He didn't like me to stare. Maybe the eye patch disturbed him, although he'd been a surgeon and the thought of the empty orbit underneath wouldn't have made him squeamish. To be fixed by an underling's gaze, like a pin through an insect specimen, must have annoyed him. What insect most resembled Durant? The cicada-killing wasp. And me? One that crawled about in muck and seemed to be at home in it. The idea of beauty lay far off for me. The gulf between that "rough sketch" of a man in a white suit and the person who would winter in the Wasatch with the Ute is as wide as the

Pacific Ocean, which I would glimpse, once, like Moses did the Promised Land. No, I could not have said then what beauty meant. Nor could I have explained what it meant to be human. Six years after that summer night in 1868, I would have my picture taken, sitting, like a desert sheikh, on the hump of a Custer-dispatched buffalo where it lay in terrifying silence on the grass. I was a coward even then.

"In the fifties, I was involved in the construction of the Rock Island Railroad," said Durant. "I hired Lincoln to defend a new bridge against a suit brought by riverboat operators claiming it was a hazard to navigation. They demanded that the bridge, the first to carry track across the Mississippi, be taken down, after the steamer *Effie Afton* ran into it. Abe was a long-shanked, raw-boned, wiseacre Springfield attorney then. Like me, he believed in America's western expansion across the Mississippi and on to the Pacific and in railroads as the thing to accomplish it. Riverboat companies, which had been fattening on the north-south trade, didn't see it that way. Lincoln won the case — *Hurd vs. Rock Island Bridge Company* — by arguing it brilliantly. Many people had a low opinion of Lincoln's brains; some still do.

But if they'd seen him in the courtroom that day, they'd have had their minds changed. Honest Abe was shrewd and ruthless when he had to be. He'd fight tooth and nail if you cornered him. I admired the man and the lawyer. You know, Stephen, there were two reasons I hired you: first, because of General Grant's push; second, because you played a part in Lincoln's send-off."

He smiled benevolently. He might have patted me on the shoulder had there not been a polished mahogany bar between us. Encouraged, I seized the opportunity to ask him a favor. One succeeds in business, as in war, by taking advantage of an enemy's weak moment. And if robber barons were in the habit of getting what they wanted, Durant might respect a young man for going brazenly after what *he* wanted.

"I have a proposition for you, Dr. Durant." I thought he might overlook an upstart's ambition if I couched my request in terms as familiar to an entrepreneur as a Hail Mary is to a Catholic.

"A proposition. Is that right?"

I detected amusement in his tone, and, emboldened, I continued: "I'd like you — that is, the railroad — to set me up as a photographer. I can use a corner of the tool car, next to my bunk, for a darkroom. Any photographs I make will be Union Pacific property."

"Do you know how to make a photograph?"

His two eyes bore into my one good one like a pair of hot gimlets. If any power on earth could have grown me a new eyeball, it would have been Durant's stare. I felt my insides clench, like a case of the gripe, and my poor bunghole pucker. For once, I kept my gaze fixed and unwavering on his, so as not to appear shifty. Now was not the time for servility. I wished I had on my own clothes — my Union blues, for preference, if I hadn't given them away — instead of a weaseling steward's uniform. Chen was right: It did make me look like a bottle of milk.

"Have you ever taken one?" Durant asked.

"No, sir." Honesty, my instincts told me, was the best card to play. "But I watched that newspaper fellow up on the hundredth meridian, and there didn't seem much to it. I'm sure I can teach myself how and then take you some swell pictures of railheads, tracks, and scenery on the way to Ogden."

He grew silent, letting his attention drift to the carriage windows, which the pitch-dark night outside had turned into mirrors. In one of them, I saw on his face the stricken look of a man who all of a sudden finds himself in a place he doesn't recollect and can't explain how he got there. I let him be awhile. The rambunctious Wyoming wind whipped and buffeted the car as though it meant to topple it. I felt lonely. A man who comes to the end of the world, with night and nothingness at his back, would feel like this. It came to me with a jolt how isolated we two were in our candlelit car, with only the huddles of miners' camps, sod huts, and miserable Indian villages between us and the civilized world on the far side of the Mississippi. If I were to climb one of the limestone hills that shone faintly up near the rising moon, I wondered if I would see — faraway to the east — a lightening of the sky in token of broad pavements thronged by men and women and cobbled streets noisy with traffic in the gaslit cities of Chicago, St. Louis, and New York.

I'd spent my life in crowds — in Brooklyn and Manhattan, Washington City and Omaha, and on fields where blue- and gray-coated dead men were in the majority. But there was solace even in that, poor as it was, for the dead can be company when you have no other.

My life didn't end among granite peaks,

on a solitary length of track, but I would never again sense so vast an emptiness. It belonged to the Lakota — that emptiness — granted them in perpetuity. They were welcome to it. Only an Indian would live in desolation, without so much as a telegraph wire to bear witness to enlightenment and progress. That changed after Custer's Black Hills Expedition. Having once been deemed worthless and therefore fitting for savages, the Black Hills would become the Gum Sham the Chinese had dreamed of finding. Only they had no more right to it than the Indians cast out from what had been given them "for as long as grass grows and rivers run." What did an Indian want with a precious metal, when he'd be just as happy with a tin can — or a bottle, preferably full of rum? Such was the general opinion and, to be truthful, mine. It would take time and experience before I could rise above the common view, tarred and mired with it as I'd been since my tenement days. With us, hatred was a staple we'd gnaw on, like a dog a bone. It might have lacked nourishment, but it kept the teeth sharp. Of all the people I knew in childhood, only my mother managed to make room in her generous heart for whoever or whatever needed comforting.

"If you can stake me," I said, rounding to my proposition, "I'll undertake to be the Union Pacific's photographer."

The candles had guttered to nothing. The car was awash with night. The pine, spruce, aspen, and birch trees clinging to the steep hills might have lengthened their aboriginal shadows down the face of the butte, across the high country, and into the opulent carriage where Death's own shadow had lain for twelve nights — so very black it was. Durant hadn't stirred the whole time my mind milled what grist the night and its terrors brought. Scared, I determined to break the silence, though it cost me my camera.

"Dr. Durant," I said in a whisper of a voice.

He didn't answer. I felt an oppression of the chest as disquiet gave way to dismay.

"Dr. Durant, are you all right?" I said, louder this time, though not so very loud, in case my voice should break into a shout that could shiver the china cups: an uncanny sound to stop the heart of a young man of nineteen, surrounded by darkness, who felt at that instant like the last person left on earth.

I picked up the knife I used to shuck oysters. Little good it would do me against fiends or the ghosts of murdered Indians.

Then I heard Durant — I couldn't see him in the dark. He caught his breath, snuffled like a wasp in a jam pot, and began to snore: a soft and even rasp that made the bedeviled carriage ordinary again. The terror that had nearly finished me vanished. I let him sleep and gave up all hope of prying a camera out of a millionaire. Like all of his kind, he held that the audacity of having staked all entitled him to take all, without a downward pitying glance at those who lost or lacked the sand to try.

I tried to imagine Durant's dreams. Did he see visions of railroads, gilt-edged securities (guilt-edged is more like it), *nymphs du prairie* in shimmies and fancy drawers, slinking about a Denver bordello? Or was he once more in Lee, Massachusetts, in the summer of 1830, when his childish ambition extended no further than a fish hook at the end of a line? How little we know of life! Once before, I'd felt the earth swinging to no purpose through a space hostile to humankind. That time also involved a man waiting, motionless, in the dark of this same silent coach. Afraid to wake him — Durant's temper could be sharp when he was abruptly roused — I closed my eye and fell into the chasm of sleep.

I was sweeping out the private car when a black boy knocked at the door. He took off his hat, handed me a folded piece of paper, and ran off without a word. Lincoln and war had freed the slaves, but the habits of abjection were too ingrained to be broken in a generation. They waited, excitable as Fleischmann's yeast, to rise and show themselves. A scowl or an angry word could make a Negro doff his cap to a white woman or step aside to let a white man pass. Black folk might have been disenthralled, but their fear remained — with good reason. For no sooner had the war ended than six disgruntled rebs cut eye holes in their missuses' sheets. Rope became a thing with which to hang a man, and crosses, such as the lynched Jesus had sanctified, a torch to burn in a black sharecropper's yard. Traffickers in human sweetness — the poets, preachers, and printers of Valentine's Day cards — declare love to be our kind's supreme emotion. Young as I was, I suspected enmity held sway.

The note asked if I would come to the Jackson Brothers' photographic studio at three o'clock that afternoon, "if convenient."

You can call William Henry Jackson's arrival in Omaha "triumphal" insofar as a cowboy whooping and waving his dusty Stetson to goad a herd of exasperated cattle into the stockyard, at the end of a thousand-mile trail through hostile territory, has completed a journey as harrowing and as worthy of commemoration as Ulysses' or Hannibal's. Heroic moments like Jackson's belong to the mythology of the West — the Old West now, in 1901.

William came West in '66, with Gettysburg and jobs as a photographer's assistant behind him. Before he and his brother Edward opened their Omaha studio, William had tried his hand not only at cow-poking but also at silver mining and bull whacking on a mule train bound for Montana. He left it in Wyoming and made his way to Salt Lake City, where the Mormons were building their temple near the River Jordan to honor the angel Moroni. Burton, the Victorian explorer and adventurer, must have considered the city as fantastic as Lake Tanganyika or Mecca and the Mormons as exotic as *The Arabian Nights* to have traveled there six years before. By the time William reached California, his infatuation with picture making had been revived by the alien grandeur of the scenery. The West made his home state of Vermont look like a picnic grove.

The afternoon when I walked into the Jackson Brothers' studio, William was up on the Missouri River, making stereopticon views of the Pawnee. Sated with photographs of the Civil War, eastern voyeurs clamored for novelty; and photographers who had been fixing images of fratricide on glass-plate negatives could no longer sell them, except as panes for greenhouses, where — bleached by an indifferent sun — they proved less than indelible. Thus, in time, are the most horrifying events forgotten as history fades and disappears. Having lumbered by mule or wagon from one corpse-strewn battlefield to another, Gardner, O'Sullivan, Pywell, and others of the wet-plate sodality were now out shooting the Western Territories — their native peoples and natural splendors, along with an itinerant population of miners, drovers, teamsters, hunters, trappers, hucksters, gamblers, whores, soldiers, renegades, bad men, and "characters." W. H. Jackson, as he styled himself, became famous for recording the authentic life and likenesses of Pawnee, Osage, Otoe, Winnebago, and Omaha Indians before they were erased ("chalked over" would be more apt) by the strong arm of history. History is what gets written by the conquerors, but in the end, it's just so much dust. Paper molders, ink dries in the bottle, and conquerors lime the dirt with their indistinguishable bones.

You'll accuse me, no doubt, of simplifying history, Jay. Most of us do just that, knowing no more of it than our own time — and not knowing even that much well and truly.

Edward Jackson stayed behind in the Omaha studio, taking pictures of whoever walked through the door in hopes of cheating time. When I walked through it at three o'clock, with wet leaves pasted to my soles, he was immortalizing the wife of one of the Sheely brothers, who looked like one of their own sausages. I guess she had as much right to immortality as Jenny Lind, though I doubted posterity or the heirs to the Omaha packinghouse fortune would care to dwell on her portrait. Edward emerged from the camera's black drape, counted to twenty, and capped the lens. I wondered if an exposure's duration was commensurate with gross weight. If so, the "Swedish Nightingale" would need no more than a blink of light against the plate's silver-halide grains to capture her winsome figure. Edward must have been thinking along similar lines.

"There was so much of her, I needed the stereo camera," he remarked drily after the fat woman had unfurled an umbrella and, grasping an elegantly carved handle made from the horn of a steer felled in the family's own slaughterhouse, stepped outside into the puddled street.

I introduced myself while he developed and rinsed the negative. The walls of the studio were hung with democratic portraits of American types that might have stepped from the pages of Whitman's book: carpenters, masons, boatmen, mechanics, lumbermen, butchers, trappers, agents, cowboys, scouts, saloon keepers — occupations either glorious or inglorious, depending on your side of the divide between the haves and the have-nots. Edward was grimly egalitarian, like anybody who fled to the frontier after his roots had failed to take hold in his native soil.

Westering was a kind of sickness that swept over the body, a fever of the brain, a craze, a seizure, an unmooring, a tide in which people got caught up like corks in a flood. They were beside themselves with the irresistible desire to leave — to put a continent between their old lives and what they imagined would become of them if they could only emigrate. They'd become famous or infamous, according to their predisposition — or to the dictates of

Predestination, if you believe in it. Regardless, they'd — we'd — be judged deserving of honor or the noose, as if there were no hand at our backs, pushing us. And rightly so.

"Durant had your new camera shipped here so I could teach you how to use it."

Believing Durant had forgotten or dismissed the proposition I'd made him months earlier up in the Black Hills, I was staggered into speechlessness.

"Perhaps you consider instruction in such an uncomplicated instrument unnecessary," said Edward, rankled by my silence, which he misconstrued as a lofty disdain for his profession.

"No, sir; I'm just surprised is all."

I doubt Uriah Heep could have made a more convincing show of humility. But Edward was slow to dismount from his high horse. He sat it like a man with a grievance.

"Didn't you ask him to purchase you a camera?" he went on, hoping to spur me into an admission he could fault. He seemed to have taken a dislike to me — for what reason, I couldn't guess, unless he was suspicious of Durant's magnanimity. My white suit and sissified vocation might have made him wonder what sort of creature I was. And whose.

"I *did* ask him, but as my mother — of blessed memory! — used to say, 'If wishes were horses, beggars would ride.' "

Whether by invoking a dead mother or by siding with beggars, I managed to quell his hostility. He went inside the darkroom and poured warm varnish over the glass plate and set it to dry. He returned to the studio, where the rainy afternoon cast a submarine light through the high windows.

"He must be a generous man," he declared: an appraisal, which was, in Durant's case, as wide of the mark as pyrite is of gold. But I thought it best to agree with him.

"He is that, sir."

"Generous men are rare in my experience," he said grudgingly.

"In mine, too," I said, to let him know that the contents of chamber pots were more likely than manna to fall on my head; sleet, than a gentle rain from heaven.

"Do you know anything at all about photography?" he asked in the voice of a man who had been won over.

I'd never have survived my youth without a disarming, slightly fraudulent manner. I was not a con man, but I borrowed his plausible face and shrewd ways to escape thrashing. Being the universal fate of everything that would seek to rise above the common dirt, thrashing, however, is mostly inescapable.

Edward showed himself to be generous of his time and knowledge, unlike many another master of an esoteric art, who keeps its secrets close in order to lord it over the uninitiated. He disclosed with no-nonsense frankness the alchemy of light and silver that could coax the likeness of a man or mountain onto a piece of glass wet with collodion and silver nitrate and from it — through a straightforward process of developing, rinsing, fixing, washing, varnishing — onto a sheet of albumen-coated paper. In two months' time, I could make a passable portrait of a water jug or of a hunter just arrived in town after massacring bison on the Nebraska plain, capturing every individual hair of his coonskin cap, every wrinkle of his deerskin shirt and sunburned face, every particular of what made him unique among men, except for his smell, which was as strong and disagreeable as a musk ox's. In time, I came to grasp the action of light on the silver halides; but what I never understood was how the image of a man made its way across the studio's rough floor or how the facsimile of a mountain crossed leagues of prairie to light, silently as a moth, on the lens of the camera or of the eyes, for that matter. I doubted Edward knew the science of the thing — or his brother, either, off among the Indians, making portraits that would explain the red man to the white, if anything so quiet and mysterious could reconcile them when the latter was clamoring, by and large, for the former's extinction.

I'd meet William the following year at the summit. He would further my education by showing me how to make a picture under the big sky, how to vary an exposure according to the light surrounding the subject and its relative motion, and — most important — how to appraise a subject's value as a testament to human dignity or natural glory. What was not possessed of the "fat light" — an immanence that shed radiance over the world of gross matter — should be left to the portraitists of sausage-shaped ladies and their rich consorts. This final lesson, the hardest, would take some time to learn; but before my instruction could begin, our two lives — wildly divergent until now — would have to converge.

Promontory Summit, Utah Territory, May 10, 1869

I've sworn to speak the truth and not gusset it with gossip and conjecture. My visions were neither, and you should take them as Gospel. Except for them — a peep through the transom window, so to speak — I've been bound, like anyone, by the ambit of my life, although in the days of which I speak, lives tended to be packed with more occupations and places than in settled times. By the end of the Civil War, half a million people had picked up and moved across the continent and reshaped their identities while they were at it. A single life is too confining for some. The West was a theater in which they might enact the promptings of desire and so enrich themselves.

Land might have been theirs for the taking, but the cost of having forded the Missouri and toiled westward into the unknown was high. I could've said "stepped off a precipice and trusted to the air" and told the truth. For every mile of the two-thousand-mile Oregon Trail — blazed in dust and salt, snow and sorrow — from Independence to the Humboldt or up into the Columbia Basin, ten graves marked the way, dug by cholera, dysentery, tuberculosis, mountain fever, snakebite, brain congestion, insanity, murder, tetanus, laudanum overdose, suicide, the high desert's entombing snows, or other misadventure. Death dealt by enraged Indians routed from tribal lands by wagon trains and cavalry was considerably less than anyone supposed. But I'll leave facts and figures to the writers of history. It's enough for a man to keep his own books. My purpose is to account for my time aboveground, whose parentheses enclose the year of my birth in 1848 and that of my death in 1901. I can see by your face you don't expect me to live out the year. Don't look so stricken, Jay! There's no need; I've lived a crowded life.

I told you how the rails of the Union Pacific and the Central Pacific met finally in the spring of '69, in Utah, near Ogden. What I recall of it (a historic moment that inaugurated the settlement and the ruination of the West), I've already said — except for my first encounter with William Jackson. I'll tell you about that meeting, which would set my life going on a new track.

Able photographers were recording the "bond of iron, which is to hold our glorious country in one eternal union," on their glass-plate negatives. Theirs would be the steel-engraved views printed in newspapers, on stereopticon cards, and, in years to come, in the history books that would revere the tenth of May, 1869, as an American holy day, when Manifest Destiny was sanctified by money and technology. The Indians of the Great Plains and the bedraggled bison that grazed there would have cause to execrate it. But who was there at Promontory Summit to care for the well-being of either? Not Durant and not the Central Pacific's president, Leland Stanford, who had gone to California in '52 and, unlike the Chinese, discovered Gum Sham in the miners' misery from which he profited. And who is there to care when time — friend of those chosen by natural selection — will have disposed of species judged unfit to survive? What the weak and the meek inherit is Oblivion.

William Henry Jackson had little interest in the ceremony of industry and progress enacted at Promontory Summit — frankincense and myrrh replaced by the profane stink of whiskey and sweat. Had he been there, Whitman would have been driven mad by his rough camerados. Jackson had already made enough icons of light and shadow to satisfy Durant, who'd hired him instead of me as the Union Pacific photographer. I held no resentment for either man, knowing Jackson to be the master of the art I now wished to practice, if only in a small way. Months in the studio with his brother had showed me how far I'd have to travel to be anything more than an apprentice. When I first laid eye on William, he had turned his camera toward a pyramid of rock, reminiscent of Giza's, rising from the horizon, well beyond the giddy jamboree. At twenty-seven minutes past two, when Stanford and Durant let fall their hammers to drive home the ceremonial spikes, the two locomotives that, until that instant, had existed as the potential of an idea for the transformation of America became the embodiment of an energy as ferocious as the atom's, unleashed in 1945 in the Jornado del Muerte.

Patience, Jay! All will be revealed in time, as it was for me by Crazy Horse. I've been as likely to misunderstand what I saw and heard as the next human. But I believe in Crazy Horse's dreams. Stanford and Durant, by the way, both missed their gold spikes, in a moment of low comedy not conveyed to San Francisco or Washington by the laconic message telegraphed from the wedding of the rails: "Done."

Lincoln had pushed the completion of the

transcontinental railroad. He thought it would strengthen the Union by speeding the incorporation of territories west of the Mississippi and help heal the nation after war. On the map, the nineteen hundred miles of track from California to Council Bluffs look like an ugly scar cut across the belly of the West, as if whatever was waiting to be born of all that money and travail had to be wrested from the Great Mother's womb. Indians believed she died of it, and all that was nourished by her generous belly and tits — the plenitude of milk and honey that had made the aboriginal land a paradise — died afterward. From what I've seen with my own eye and in the dreams sent me, the Indians were right.

That night, I went to Jackson's tent to introduce myself. He was absorbed in a negative he'd made that afternoon of the jagged peaks in the distance. I watched him pore over the eight-by-ten-inch plate, one eye squinting through a jeweler's loupe.

"There's an advantage to having just the one eye," he said, making no other overture to the stranger who'd entered his tent without invitation. He hadn't looked up. He appeared to take no notice of me in the uncertain light of the kerosene lamp, yet he'd seen enough to know I wore an eye patch. My face must have showed my amazement, like that of someone who's witnessed a parlor trick he can't explain. "One eye makes it easy to look through the camera or glass," he said, putting down his loupe on the trestle table. "And you'll never have to squint to consider some small detail of the picture."

"How did you know I want to take pictures?" I asked, under the influence of his uncanny performance.

"I saw you watching me during the high jinks this afternoon. You were too intense for someone with only a casual interest in the 'mysteries' of the profession. Although the mystery has been debunked by familiarity, and a photographer isn't the curiosity he used to be in the days of the daguerreotypist, when a crowd would gather just to see his head vanish behind the black drape. We were considered magicians then. But after a million views, the novelty's worn off."

His glance swept the negatives laid on the table and then lifted to take me in. I found his eyes hard to meet. But I did meet them, impudently, as if he were himself a photographic subject about to be pierced by the camera's all-seeing lens.

"I know who you are."

"Who?" I said sharply and much annoyed.

Jackson liked to be mystifying, the same as anyone who conjures. But my admiration was enough to satisfy him. I didn't need to truckle — he'd have hated me for it. From the first, I sensed that his pride was not in himself but in his gifts, which he willingly shared with those who treated them seriously. If he'd tried to lord it over me, I'd have turned on my heel and left — never mind that I needed him. His brother had nothing more to teach me. Already, I knew I wanted to make pictures of real things and real people — not prettifying portraits of flowers or "stiffs," which was how Edward referred to customers whose rigid poses were as lifelike as the dead men's he was sometimes asked to photograph.

"Stephen Moran," he said with a becoming smile. He laughed, and then he admitted that Edward had wired him to expect a visit from me at the summit, if I had the nerve. "My brother's been writing to me about you. He says you've the makings of a first-class photographer."

Those words gave me more pleasure than anyone else's had up to that time, not forgetting General Grant's when he gave me my medal. Just so you know, I only wore it twice after he sent it back to me. And when I outgrew my Union sack coat, I gave it to an Indian, who used to slink around Omaha buttoned up in it, begging for liquor.

"So tell me, Moran: Why do you want to be a photographer?"

He would ask that question several times during the nearly two years we traveled together. I don't think my answers ever satisfied him completely.

"You can tell a lot about your subject by studying the negative," he said, holding it to the light again.

I kept silent, knowing I was about to receive my first master lesson in the photographic — some say "art," others, "science." I began by thinking it the former; in time, I came to think of it as a science; lately, I've come to consider it a faith. Jackson handed me the glass plate. I held it to the light and studied it with my one good eye.

"Tell me what you see."

"A mountain range in the distance. In the foreground, a group of white tents. Emptiness in between."

"Good. But you must learn to look deeper."

He spoke almost gently. If he'd been sharp, the shell where my raw self resided like an oyster would have broken. You'd have thought the tender organ of someone without a childhood would quickly become hardened. But I possessed the child's eager and easily wounded heart. In my lifetime, I'd been shown little enough kindness, except by my mother, who died too soon to fortify me against the meanness of the world. It weakened me, but it did not undo me. I could be as cruel as the world is. To use a figure from a later time, I was resistant, like a virus that fire and ice ought to annihilate but can't in spite of its insignificance.

"What do I see?" I asked in a tone of voice that bespoke not servility, but the disciple's acceptance of criticism. I was twenty — the age when boys feel themselves licensed to rebel against authority. But I was ready to be chastened. I wanted to follow him into the wilderness.

"You see the invisible made visible," he uttered with the solemnity of a Hindu swami. "Moran, you see the bones of the world."

I had no idea what he meant — and wouldn't until I saw *Hand mit Ringen,* the first X-ray picture, taken by Wilhelm Röntgen of his wife's hand, in an 1897 issue of *Scientific American.*

"If you're interested only in recording the scenery, I don't have time to waste on you."

I felt as though I were picking my way through a field of Confederate "torpedoes." A misstep would nip my prospects in the bud. Already I sensed that photography could be about something more important than stiffs or scenery, but I couldn't have put it into words — not then or this morning, so many years later. Once in a great while and mostly by accident, I'd glimpse the quicksilver thing that Jackson sought with his camera; but I never caught on, you see, never really understood the spiritual thing he was after. My instincts were good; my technique was sound. I could capture a subject down to its broken shirt button and the mole in the shadow of the jaw, but for all my virtuosity, the life was no more than a facsimile. The picture wasn't dead; neither was it alive. It lacked . . . vitality. No, I was never more than a second-rate cameraman. I had sense to know, however, that my future depended on the success of my catechism. I had not the slightest idea why this should be, but I was right. Jackson was waiting for an answer (it was a question he'd left hanging in the air, even if he hadn't framed it as one), but I had none to give.

"Some pictures make me restless," I said after having temporized as long as I dared by fingering an earlobe and snuffling. The air inside the tent was pungent with chemicals.

"Restless?" His voice seemed to light up.

"The pictures I like do."

"How so?"

"I can't say. I feel a sort of anticipation. An eagerness comes over me that isn't always pleasant. It's hard to put into words."

"Where do you feel it?"

"In my heart," I replied, lying.

He spat contemptuously.

"I feel it here," I said, touching myself.

Evidently, my answer pleased him. "I'll be getting off the Omaha-bound train in Wyoming. Durant wants pictures of a miners' camp for a railroad prospectus. At least, I persuaded him he does. It's all right with him if you go along as my assistant. What do you think of the idea?"

I thought it glorious and told him as much.

"We'll get off at Bear River City and pick up a string of mules for our equipment."

I did not know how to thank him — what words to use without their sounding like a hurried grace said over a growling belly. Gratitude, sincerely meant, was foreign to my nature and experience. So I said nothing. I nodded and left him to the "stark forms of existence" that we'd hunt down one hard winter in Ute country. I stepped outside into night's negative: The rails and the limestone hills and the tents shone silver with moonlight; the sky and the desert nothingness that spread around me were black. A meteor hissed across the darkness, an auspice of the American Empire and also a portent of its end. The meteor was only in my own mind; nonetheless, it made me shiver.

Bear River, Wyoming Territory, June 1869

Five mules and two equally taciturn drivers were waiting for us by the railroad grade across Bear River. The town had jumped up to accommodate railway workers, as well as the outgoing tide of emigrants traveling the Oregon and the Mormon trails. Bear River City, as it was called in recognition of a stagecoach hotel, hash house, depot, mining office, drinking, gambling, and whoring palace, and newspaper, came to an abrupt end in the riot of November 19, 1868, sparked by a vigilante lynching. A faction sympathetic to the lynched man hunted down the vigilantes, the jailhouse was stormed, plenty of men — good and bad — were killed, and the town was torched. By the time the army put down the insurrection, the town was dead. It was often that way for would-be towns from the Platte River to the Klondike. There was a violent, lawless strain in those who itched after gold or land or a loose and large manner of living. Doubtless, the germ has been inherited, according to the mysterious workings of genetics, by people who believe in doing as they please.

Miners and hunters continued to camp at the ruined town on their outbound journeys. For some people, outbound is the only direction they know, whether the journey leads across prairie grass, desert sand, polar ice, or seawater. I was the same — never stopping after I'd left Brooklyn till I fetched up in Lincoln, like a rolling stone or a shell beached by the tide. Things have voices to tell their stories; you've only to listen to a conch shell, the wind in tall grass, the humming of a telegraph wire in falling snow, or the throbbing of a railroad track. I imagine even stones complain of bad weather, old age, and ill treatment to anything with sense enough to listen. Well, I have the right to speak my piece, the same as any stone!

Jackson liked the desperate look of the place, though I saw nothing to recommend it but charred timber frames and rocks lying where they'd fallen after having done their work as walls.

"Tell me what you see, Moran," he said while he coated a glass plate with collodion outside the darkroom tent.

I hadn't begun to see in a landscape what a camera had the power to distill. If I took a good picture — one worth all the trouble of hauling the ponderous apparatus, heavy plates, and chemicals up mountains, across rivers, and through snowdrifts and of spending the better part of an hour to prepare the wet plate, expose the negative, and fix the image — it would be by accident. For a long while, that's what it would be for me, who lacked the gift of someone like William H. Jackson. But by dint of patient repetition, I would learn, in time, to catch a little of the light that even the most stolid rock formation shed onto particles of silver. While I burned to be like him, I'd have to be satisfied with that "little." As I said, I'd never be more than second-rate, though I flatter myself I was more able than most to get at the germ of the picture. At the start, however, I had ambition. That surprises you, doesn't it, Jay? I aspired to be an adept like Jackson. In time, I'd come to realize my limitations.

"It's places like this," said Jackson, "where the eye can see plainly. "Put that one eye of yours to work, Moran, and tell me what you see in front of you."

He tossed a dried apricot into his mouth and chewed.

"I see a pile of rocks, blackened joists and studs, a stand of trees, and, down in the ravine, the river."

"Good," he said, and left me to work out for myself what made them attractive.

He took three views that afternoon while the mules chewed grass and the skinners sat, unspeaking, on a log, passing a bottle of spirits back and forth. Later, they made up a fire and cooked the cornmeal and bacon mush favored by Johnny Rebs in the recent war, which had laid waste much of the old America. Raw emotions, undignified and unadorned by noble causes, had scorched *this* earth. Could I have articulated my thoughts, I'd have asked Jackson what he saw through his camera lens of the simmering passions of men, buried still in the ruins of Bear River City.

Instead, I asked, "What does Durant want with pictures of a wrecked town?"

"He doesn't. I'm the one who wants them. Not everything's for hire, Moran. Maybe what's best in a man, he gives away."

Jackson could be as mystifying as Ralph Waldo Emerson, and his riddles annoyed the hell out of someone like me, who thought things were already mysterious enough.

The next morning, we drove the mules eight miles up Bear River, following a trail along the ravine until it came down to a ramshackle mining camp. A yellow field of goldenrod lay, dazzling, on the narrow river's opposite shore, as if to mock the lust for gold nuggets that had spurred two dozen or so men to rough it on the southwestern Wyoming plain. Standing in river water, they brought to mind Whitman, up to his knees in Sheepshead Bay. How many years ago was it? Nine. Nine years since I was a boy who had ventured no farther from his place in the world than Hell Gate or the Battery. In nine years, I'd gone south by steamboat, traipsed through Virginia, Maryland, and Pennsylvania, and ridden the rails from Washington City to Ogden, Utah. Now here I was, in a hardscrabble miners' camp in what was called the Great American Desert (a desolation bearing no resemblance to the Sahara), without even the Union Pacific tracks to remind me of civilization.

I wondered what the sum of so variegated an experience might mean to what lay inside me, bullying like a sergeant major or coaxing like a woman used to getting her own way. Was there a germ, some indissoluble particle of being that could not be misled, tempted, or turned aside from the thing that made me different from a bug? I never thought much about the soul and, like most soldiers, considered virtue a seal put on young girls, destined to be broken by sweet talk or rough ardor. Virtue was a quality as useless in a man as tits on a hog. That's not to say some of us didn't believe in goodness. Only we called it "square dealing" or "being on the level." When we said a man was "true," we weren't referring to an abhorrence of lies, but to an alignment with the common purpose or the common good (which is not the same as goodness, a quality possessed, or not, by an individual), as though a man — or a woman — were no more than a machine shaped and operating according to plan.

The hardest thing in the world to understand is one's own self. I'm not sure I ever sounded to the bottom of mine. Even now, when I have time to consider what I've been and what I am, I doubt I comprehend my humanity, if I can claim so grand a word for my own morsel of life. I might as well be a meteor as a man, for all the difference I've made on earth.

Jackson walked down to the river and spoke to a group of men working a rocker box, a kind of sieve to separate gold dust and the occasional nugget from the "placer," a shoal of black gravel runoff near the riverbank. Upstream, other knots of dirty, ragged men paid rapt attention to rocker boxes of their own — "cradles," as they were commonly called, though I never heard a lullaby sung in their vicinity. Whether by pan, sluice, or cradle, placer mining is brutal on the hands and back. For every miner who leaves the goldfield rich, a hundred others give up and go home, with less to show for their toil than an asparagus cutter's wages. Prospectors are a half-crazed, harum-scarum, mostly unhappy lot, who no longer dream of the things they meant to buy with their dust, but only of its extraction. These men were nothing like Bret Harte's Stumpy or Kentuck; the Bear River digs, a far cry from Roaring Camp, where a rosewood cradle was hauled eighty miles by mule to comfort the foundling Tommy Luck.

Jackson returned, and we set up the tent and readied plates to reproduce, with a ray of light on glass, the gruff and crusty miners. We exposed three negatives the first day and five the next: of men at the cradles, sifting black gravel; eating game and turnip stew washed down with black coffee and rum; sitting in their tents, their tired faces reddened by the setting sun. Only four of the plates were "good enough for Durant" — meaning that the miners had sat still long enough to make their likenesses sharp, while their lifelike quality was drained by the rigor mortis of a lengthy exposure.

"These are for me," said Jackson, pensively regarding four of the glass negatives, where the faces or some other aspect of the photograph lay in darkness or a hand was caught in motion — a blur of human anatomy caused by a restless subject. Jackson gazed at them as though they were gold and the others — for Durant's lithographed prospectus — the worthless gravel dumped from a rocker box.

I confess I didn't see the beauty of those spoiled views.

"Sometimes the truth is revealed when taken by surprise," he said in that infuriating way of his.

"Your brother would have goddamned them as a waste of chemicals and glass."

"Edward confuses art with perfection. Never despise the blemish, Moran,"

I was tired and had had enough lessons for one day. My outdoor technique was being refined under Jackson's tutelage; I had skinned the time it took me to coat a glass with collodion and expose it before it began to dry. I'd begun to "read the light," which is more changeable and elusive under the big sky than inside the studio. I was pleased with myself and in no mood to be nettled by Jackson's metaphysics. I sometimes wonder if he missed his calling as a philosopher or a theologian — but damn if he didn't make some of the most gorgeous images of any I would ever see! In my lifetime, I would learn to take respectable photographs. When I began sending them to Whitman, he wrote to say how fine they were and how what I'd learned to see of the West insinuated itself into his poems. That was praise enough.

Early next morning, I loaded a mule with my camera and darkroom tent and walked upriver about a mile from camp. There, I found George Osler, one of the Bear River miners, originally from Pennsylvania. He was dangling a length of cord from a cut branch into the dark water; on the end of it was a drowned worm threaded on a hook.

"Morning," he said as I tied the mule to a cottonwood.

"Morning," I said. "Fishing?"

"There's an almighty catfish down there, but I'm too lazy to catch him."

He nodded toward the river, whose bed lay below what the slant of early-morning light through the cottonwoods could illuminate. It occurred to me that a fish unseen on the bottom, dragged up into sunlight, was like a truth surprised into revelation; but the warm June morning was too fine to bother with extravagant notions. I gave myself up to the pleasure of watching an angler enjoying his idleness, without any real ambition to complicate it by extricating the hook from the mouth or throat of a catfish, whose fins can cut a finger to ribbons and inject a dose of venom as painful as a water moccasin bite. He was one of those people who enjoy their pastimes in the abstract. Something stirred in the roots of a willow dug into the muddy bank. I turned in time to see a muskrat jump and disappear beneath the water. When I looked back at Osler, he was raising a monstrous fish, apparently unconcerned by either my opinion of his zeal or the danger of catfish even at their last gasp.

"It's a humdinger!" he said, admiring the fish juddering in the grass. "It's almost worth the effort to have caught him."

He put his boot on the creature's flank and worked out the hook. Seeing the worm none the worse for its ordeal, I felt the poor fish had been cheated. By rights, it ought to have enjoyed the temptation that proved to be its undoing. I supposed there was a moral lesson to be learned from this small tragedy, a fable of some kind, but the sun made me too lazy to decipher it. Osler's purpose was far from didactic, however. He brained the fish, slit it from gills to anus, pulled out its entrails, and rinsed it in the river.

"Had your breakfast yet?" he asked.

I had, but I was curious about the taste of a catfish flavored by Bear River.

"No, and I can feel my belly rubbing up against my backbone."

He made up a fire and spitted the heavy fish on a barked stick. In short order, the skin was bubbling with its own hot juices. We sat down on the grass and ate — the white flesh tasting of river. I enjoyed that breakfast out on the Wyoming scrubland more than any fancy meal I'd eaten on the train. When it was finished, I cursed myself aloud for having forgotten to take a picture of the occasion. It would have been worth showing Jackson: the morning light picking out every reddish whisker of the miner's stubble, the coals of the fire, the fish, its mouth gaping open on the spit, the river behind, and, behind it, a stand of ponderosa pines stuck up, stiff and sharp, against the wide-open sky.

"I'll show you a sight for picture taking," said Osler, wiping grease from his lips onto the back of his hand. His hand was interesting: scarred and bulging with blue veins, the nails black and broken.

We walked about three hours, across prairies and over low hills. I led the mule packed with my equipment. I think we crossed into Utah, but I can't swear to it. I was dazed by the big sky, which had lost its awful clarity now that the wind was herding clouds from west to east, casting woolly shadows on the leaning grass. Like most of his kind, Osler was not given to idle conversation. I don't know what silences such men. They're not contemplative: They don't look into themselves. Maybe they're struck dumb by the spectacle of untrammeled nature. Maybe they exist on a level of consciousness where speech is neither habitual nor desirable. He said little until we came through a defile and out onto a wide prairie.

"There," he said tersely, nodding toward a complicated lathwork of bones that sprawled into the bluish distance like a street of houses going up.

"What the hell?" I nearly shouted with the shock of what I'd come upon in the grass.

"Go and see."

"You coming?"

"I already saw. I'll wait here." He sat on the grass and busied himself with his pipe and tobacco.

I got up onto the mule and nudged its flanks. It didn't budge. I kicked at the recalcitrant animal, and it started forward, its back hooves clattering nervously against fieldstone. The wind pushed a lumbering cloud across the face of the sun, and the bones, which an instant before had been slashes of fierce light, darkened. The mule shied, whinnied, and heehawed. I whipped it, with an anger I didn't understand. I suppose what provoked me and agitated the poor beast was fear. The soughing of the tall grass couldn't be heard for the flies, as loud and insolent as they'd been four years earlier in the Armory Square Hospital's bedpans. I held down my rising gorge, unwilling to let the older man see me unnerved.

Maybe he sensed my discomfiture, because he stood up and walked the thirty yards or so separating us. He stroked the mule's quivering flank and murmured to quiet it. I was grateful for the smell of his tobacco smoke and for the noise of the embers when he drew on the pipe. The mule calmed under his hand.

"Told you it was a sight," he said.

The steppe was crowded with the remains of bison — grass growing up through bones that, except for scant rags of flesh, had been picked clean and bleached.

"I never counted, but I'd guess maybe four, five hundred animals laying here. Or what used to be."

The troops sent to the Great Plains were killing buffalo in order to starve the Indians, forcing them onto reservations and away from the goldfields, settlements, and emigrant trails. It was "scorched-earth" William Tecumseh Sherman's policy and Grant's, too. The commander of Fort Dodge, where pretty-boy Custer was stationed, liked to tell the newspapers, "Every dead buffalo is one Indian gone." The government was hell-bent on exterminating both.

"I'd rather they was Indian bones any day than buffalo," Osler said, his long yellow teeth clenched on his pipe stem.

In those days, I would have agreed.

I felt bewildered and sick. At that moment, I hated the Union and its army and wished Sherman, Grant, Custer, and the whole infernal gang dead. But in my own bones, I knew it wouldn't change anything. If Davis and Lee had been victorious and the Indian Wars were being waged by men in gray, these same buffalo bones would be lying in the grass, the wind singing lamentations through the harps of their rib cages — their hides sent east on the new railroad and bought by the tanneries with Confederate money to make lap robes and mufflers. That's what people are like.

Osler spit what we called an "oyster" back in Brooklyn and asked, "Aren't you going to take a picture?"

I was transfixed by the maze of carcasses undressed of flesh by varmints, carrion birds, and industrious insects, their bones scrubbed clean by rain, the light of the harsh sun, and time. I could not take my eye off the wreckage, as though a thread of pity joined me to it.

"Seems a shame after coming all this way."

Shame. That's what this was, and shame was what I felt. Like a man who stumbles on a corpse, or like anyone who discovers a secret that makes him want to retch, to weep, to stab the sight from his eyes, to do like the ancients and tear out his hair and cover himself with dirt. For here on the desolate plain, the secret nature of our kind had been made visible in a latticework of bones. I think our shame will save us, if anything can.

I set up the tent and camera, coated a plate, and stuck my head behind the drape. But the subject matter was too big — the enormity of it — even for an eight-by-ten-inch plate. I'd need a view camera like the one used by Robert Vance to photograph the mines and prospectors of the California goldfields. No, not even that big negative could begin to capture what I saw — what I *felt* when looking at so much death. That was it: No camera could contain my feelings for the subject. The pity of it. By now, you know I was not easily moved. I had seen death parceled out wholesale during the war and retailed on the cobbled streets of lower Manhattan, and I'd never flinched. I was accustomed to heaps and piles of dead men. I'd grown a callus over the tender conscience given us at birth. Maybe I was becoming womanish in my feelings. I'd need to be careful, or the bad men of the West would devour me, would pick my bones clean.

"I shot a man once for beating his dog with a shovel," said Osler unapologetically while I pretended to read the light that glared on the bones like caustic soda.

So here, too, was someone who could be moved. A man with a modicum of respect for life — if not for a human's, then a dumb beast's. George Osler and I might have been low down on the ladder when it came to sentiment, leastways compared to Sunday school teachers, but we were a rung or two above the gunfighters, bushwhackers, claim jumpers, thieves, and cutthroats that crawled over the West like dung beetles on a steaming pile of shit.

"I can't stand to see an animal mistreated," Osler said.

In their youth, George and his brother, Frank, had a small dairy out in the country, north of Philadelphia. They'd kept a dozen milk cows and a horse to make deliveries. George talked about his family and his cows and how much he liked the life he'd had then. When I asked him why he'd left it to come west, he shrugged. I'd seen that shrug before, given in reply to the same question. Men would say, "To get a piece of land," "To get rich," "To get away from my wife and family," "To get the bit out from between my teeth," "To get closer to God," "To get out of His sight." Or they would say nothing, looking you fiercely in the eye or at thin air or the dirt at their feet. I suppose the best answer — meaning the most truthful — was the one I finally gave Jackson for wanting to take pictures: "I don't exactly know."

That day, I made two plates; the first a lengthy exposure. I wanted to capture the light on the bones, but not so that they were flooded by it. I was after that peculiar radiance Jackson called the "fat light." The second plate, I exposed twice as long to give the weakened rays of the cloud-dampened sun time to burn themselves onto the negative.

"We'll sleep here tonight," said Osler. "Too risky to travel the pass without a full moon."

I nodded and decided not to pack up the camera just yet. I thought I'd leave the lens uncovered to see how the remains would photograph under a sliver of moon and the gravel of stars. Of course, it didn't turn out: The wet plate dried during the exposure. Later, when I showed it to Jackson, expecting to be lambasted for my stupidity, he said he was pleased. He reminded me that life and pictures can happen by accident. He looked at the empty plate and declared it "beautiful." I don't believe in accidents — not anymore.

Osler took the mule and rode off toward the trees to gather wood. A June night can be cold a mile above sea level. We'd also need a fire to heat up our hash and coffee. Besides, I didn't care for the idea of sleeping among so many dead creatures. I didn't believe in what the eye couldn't see and the hand couldn't choke. Still, it's easy to see ghosts when you sleep in a graveyard. I wanted a fire to ward them off.

"I saw something even worse in the Platte River Valley," said Osler, arranging sticks of wood with the fastidiousness of a haberdasher. "A two-hundred-mile stretch of bones — bare and bleached like these here." He shook his shaggy head in wonder, as anyone might who happened on a thing so unspeakable that it defied understanding. "A man can kill eighty buffalo in a day, if he puts his mind to it."

In three years, white hunters and soldiers killed eight million American bison — not to eat, but for their hides, or for the pleasure they took in subjugating something remarkable, or for military strategy in the total war against native peoples, which were "fated to pass away" from the earth so that the Caucasian race could inherit it.

That night, Osler continued in a talkative vein. Maybe he, too, was scared. Maybe he was awed by the presence of death or the absence of life (they're not exactly the same thing). Maybe he knew that, after tomorrow, he'd never see me again. He could tell me his thoughts and admit feelings he never would to the other miners. Men seem cruelest when they are in one another's company for any length of time. He said that he and Frank had come west the year before and gotten off the train at Omaha. They hadn't been in town long when Frank got stabbed coming out of a saloon.

"By an Indian wearing a Union blue coat."

"With sergeant's stripes?" I asked. If I'd been a rabbit, my ears would have tensed in alarm.

"Yes. Know him?"

"I saw him around."

The most inconsequential thing can forge a chain of fatality: Whitman, Grant, Lincoln, Durant, Jackson, George Osler, Frank, a dispossessed, demoralized, and rum-soaked Indian — all connected by a sack coat. And that field of bones . . . is it connected to the firmament of stars? Whitman knew the truth: Everything is pitched to a mystic chord. Though not always sweetly. Such are the thoughts that come to a man in the night.

"What happened to the Indian who stabbed your brother?"

"I put a bullet in him," Osler replied.

I lay in my bedroll and watched the moon climb up a corner of the sky and start down the other side. The stars composed their ancient stories, told each night to an earth that suffers under our dominion. The bones of nine hundred Indian ponies shone under this same sliver of a moon, near the Washita River in Indian Territory, after having suffered natural processes to turn them into a ruin interesting to photographers. In November, Custer had ordered the ponies shot after his 7th Cavalry killed the Cheyenne while they slept beneath white flags raised above their tents.

Custer. He would fester in me, like a dirty splinter.

The wind had lain down with Osler and me. Now and again it rose to hymn the night, which is, as anyone knows who's slept outside in it, holier than the common day woven of distractions. If one turned out, I decided to send a print of the killing field to Grant to remind him of what death looked like, stripped of glamour and rhetoric. Sitting in his White House, he might have forgotten "the stark forms of existence."

I know what you're thinking, Jay. Your disapproval is written all over your face. Bear with me awhile longer, and then you can have your say.

Omaha, Nebraska, June–September 1870

Now that the Union Pacific was finished,

Durant had no more need of the old Lincoln parlor car or its steward. I burned my white uniform and became William Jackson's full-time assistant. I let my hair grow long and wore a beard like his, and I didn't give a damn whether my fingernails were clean or not. We lived on board the "photographic car," fitted out with berths, a trestle table, and upholstered chairs abandoned when a tent town erected along the right-of-way went bust. There was also a darkroom. I became skilled at printing negatives, retouching albumen prints, and hand-coloring stereopticon cards of the Wild West. Ordered by a Boston firm, the cards gave voyeurs back east something to gape at. It was hack work and oftentimes despicable, but Jackson depended on its income to finance his excursions.

While he was off taking pictures of Indians, I worked on the Boston job and on an album of prints for Durant, commemorating the Omaha depot. When I finished it, he handed me the camera's bill of sale. I was nearly twenty-two and considered myself disenthralled at last, as Lincoln would have said. I've often wondered whether he would have advocated extermination, like Custer and Phil Sheridan; salvation, like the missionaries; or starvation, like Sherman, as the final solution to the Indian problem. (It was by Lincoln's order that the Northern Ute were driven out of the Provo Valley onto a reservation.) Frankly, I didn't see how to pacify them. We couldn't pack them off to Africa the way we wanted to do the blacks. The Indians might have had good reason to kill us, but we couldn't just doff our hats and offer them our scalps.

In June 1870, Durant sent Jackson to Colorado Territory to photograph the linking of the Denver Pacific to the new transcontinental railroad. Afterward, Jackson traveled by stage-coach the hundred miles to Denver City, where he'd been commissioned to make portraits of the mining millionaires Tabor, Croke, Patterson, and Campbell. They paid him, as they paid for everything, ostentatiously.

"Each handed me a hundred-dollar gold piece," Jackson told me later. "Then each one lit a cigar with a hundred-dollar bill. I don't think they meant to humiliate me, only to prove to one another that they were too rich to consider such sums anything more than a trifle."

The money, along with what the recent stereopticon order brought in, would be enough to restock our plates and chemicals and to allow us to live like lords through the coming winter. Or so I thought. Jackson went out and got himself bathed, shaved, and massaged, replenished his supply of dried apricots, and bought a brand-new wool union suit for each of us at Omaha Dry Goods. The town had grown prosperous, and Geissinger, the store's squint-eyed owner, had hired a painter to add EMPORIUM in gold letters to his sign. I wondered what had possessed Jackson to buy me new underwear, but I said nothing, knowing how much he liked to appear mysterious. Jackson would have made an excellent shaman or a Moslem fakir, depending on the hemisphere.

"We're going to take a trip up into northern Utah," he said finally, chewing on an apricot.

I waited for him to elaborate, but he got into his berth without another word and shortly began to snore — the ends of his ample mustache riffling with each exhalation. I pushed a chair into the late-afternoon light and read awhile in *Leaves of Grass* — the passage beginning "O something pernicious and dread!/ Something far away from a puny and pious life!" I never failed to find a sentiment in Whitman's book that accorded with my own life and aspirations. I knew people — men and women both — who would open the Holy Bible and stab blindly at the page with a finger to find an answer in times of trouble and crisis. I would use his *Leaves,* which is, I believe, also a holy book. Doesn't he say in it about the grass "I guess it is the handkerchief of the Lord"?

Jackson woke from his nap, and we sat down to eat at the trestle table where we worked on our negatives and prints. I heated coffee and some corned beef and potatoes on the spirit lamp, filled our mugs, and flung wet gobs of hash into tin bowls. We ate in silence. Finished, Jackson pushed his bowl aside, sipped his coffee, and told me at last what he had in mind.

"I want to photograph a sorry ragtag band of Northern Ute," he said. "To get the bad taste of Denver millionaires out of my mouth."

I thought of the heavy woolen underwear and began to worry.

"When?" I asked, already knowing the answer.

"If we leave soon, we can get there before the snow piles up in the passes."

We could have traveled in relative comfort on the Utah Central from Ogden to Salt Lake City, but Jackson wouldn't hear of it.

He was sick of railroads, which, in his opinion, had tamed things, and wanted to surround himself with "the haggard beauty" of the Wasatch Range when the snow began to fall.

"Can't we go in the spring?"

He shook his head.

"Why not?"

"I want to see the Indians at their most miserable," he said.

The Utah Valley, October 1870–April 1871

The Ute gave their name to Utah, and whatever else they had of value (they owned nothing, ownership being an alien concept) — land, timber, artifacts, buffalo, elk, antelope, and deer — Utahans took. So it went anywhere Indians had, by right of prior possession, what emigrants coveted. The taking proved easy; they swarmed over Indian lands, regardless of treaties made with the "white fathers," and stole or killed what they liked. When the Indians objected, the squatters complained to the newspapers and Congress, and the army herded the Indians onto wastelands to the sentimental drinking tune of "Garry Owen." If they became indignant and scalped a few settlers or prospectors out of pique, the army retaliated by killing their men, women, and children and the millions of bison the Indians relied on for food, clothing, shelter, and spiritual well-being. Some say there were as many as 75 million buffalo on the Great Plains before we hunted them nearly to extinction to feed railroad workers toiling west, to profit from their bones and hides, to satisfy the itch to kill, and — most important — to annihilate the Lakota and the Cheyenne. Unable to defeat them, the army eventually starved them into submission.

Jackson and I entered the Utah Valley through the Wasatch. *Wasatch* is Ute for "low pass over high range." He hadn't anticipated the quantity of snow fallen already in the mountain passes, and the going was arduous, exhausting us as well as the mules, which found their footing with difficulty on the snow-covered rocks. We spent six days on the crossing, made increasingly nervous by each day's new snowfall. It was bitter, and the raw wind cut. I recalled the fate of the Donner Party in the Sierra Nevada two decades earlier and wondered how Jackson would taste, stuffed with his dried apricots.

I never doubted I could endure the extremities of weather and terrain. I spent four years living like an animal in mud, rain, snow, and heat. And a tenement in winter or in the dog days is far worse. I'd survived an impoverished childhood and a terrifying war, but trudging through the Wasatch passes took the sand out of me. I felt my backbone melt in the heat of Sisyphean exertion, and — no sooner had it turned to slurry — I'd wince as it froze up once more in the cold. Forlorn, I would spend bitter hours of repentance for having agreed to make a trip for no other reason than to take pictures of the "fish eaters," the Toompahnahwach Ute wintering in misery on the shore of Utah Lake. Jackson was imperturbable. Not even frostbitten toes could discourage him. He would spend the better part of his life in strange countries, including the one found inside each of us, and never doubt himself or yield to self-pity, the latter a quality predominant in my character.

On the seventh day, we came out of the snow-bandaged mountains and into the valley, near the Mormon settlement at Spanish Fork, about ten miles south of Provo. After resting the mules and giving them a ration of provender, we rode west toward the big lake where the fish eaters had their winter camp.

There were fifty-three Toompahnahwaches

— call them Ute, for convenience — living under shabby lice-infested buffalo hides stretched on alder saplings. How lice managed to survive their wretchedness became a theme I returned to often that winter. In my boredom, I'd speculate on the damnedest things: how geese knew when to step up onto the ice before lake water knit up around them; why piss didn't freeze in our bladders, when we couldn't lick a metal spoon without our tongues sticking to it; why our stubble didn't stay, by some kind of natural law, inside our faces, where it would be warmed, at least a little, by our blood — questions of no great import, inspired by the cold. I would have felt sorry for the Indians if I hadn't been busy feeling sorry for myself. The snow crackled, hissed, and seethed; it twisted, wraithlike, over the white crust when the wind grumbled. What birds we hadn't eaten shivered on the ridgepole. By the time April came and, with it, the thaw, nine Indians had perished from a variety of ills: children, old people, and a girl. One child was born and survived — a fact I consider miraculous under circumstances that were worse than dire.

Jackson exposed only a dozen negatives that winter. He would prepare the glass plates inside a darkroom tent, warmed by an amber-shaded spirit lamp; but the collodion thickened in the open air and the light grew sluggish as the views of lake and frozen steppe were closed down by falling snow. His hands, chilled to uselessness, would fumble among his glass plates and chemicals like those of a blind man desperate to touch what was familiar. The negatives he did manage were made during the hour or two when the sun seemed to rally with a yellowy light reminiscent of an egg yolk; usually, it looked pale as a pearl on the steely blue or leaden sky above the snow-scabbed lake. That's a purple passage fit for a novel but hardly descriptive of the actuality of that winter, which was almost past enduring. They were discouraging times even for Jackson.

He was someone used to looking at the world through a lens — it was his eye — and he relied on his instrument to sound the depths of his subject matter, whether it was a formation of rocks or a solitary Indian. Unable to photograph the Ute as often as he'd like that winter, Jackson tried to "see" them without his camera. Two of the old men could speak English and did so with an eloquence that made me think of the King James Bible or Lincoln's speeches. They'd been civilized by Quakers who had come all the way from Pennsylvania to turn them from heathens into gents. They could read and write and had sent polite letters to Johnson and Grant, asking that the government respect its treaties and allow the Ute to keep their buffalo herds safe from the hunters paid to slaughter them. Otherwise, there'd be nothing left but roots, bark, and vermin between them and starvation. Naturally, the government ignored them.

Jackson would spend hours palavering with the pair of natives, learning to "read the Indian," just as he read the light, while I sat in a corner of the lodge, wrapped in stinking buffalo hides, sulking, speculating, and experimenting with my spit. I wanted to see if I could launch a gob high enough so that it would freeze in midair. I was in no mood to understand the black and unfathomable hearts of savages.

But something happened in February to change me; some would say for the better, though most would say to the detriment of my immortal soul. I took up with an Indian girl. I hesitate to say I fell in love with her, although if I'm honest, that is what I did — at least as I understand the term.

She had one of those comical Indian names like Sparks Blown up a Chimney. Hers was Fire Briskly Burning. I can't recall what it was in Ute. Aptly named, she'd start up in my hands like a brush fire. We spoke not a word of each other's languages. That was fine with me. I left the conversing to Jackson. He had a wife, in Omaha. He could enlarge his mind on the shore of Utah Lake all he wanted. I was lonely and happy enough just to be in Fire's arms. I didn't need to visit her country every time my blood was up, and during those dismal months underneath her buffalo robes, we congressed only half a dozen times or so. Mainly, I was after her warmth. No, I didn't use her like a hot brick you take to bed on a winter's night, although people who sleep in pairs know what a furnace a human being is. No, not just for that, anyway. I wanted to be close to another person — a woman, by preference. It didn't matter whether she spoke Ute or Creole, Egyptian or Chinese. Maybe the isolation of that outpost on the ragged edge of nothingness made me crazy. Only once before had I felt as empty: when I watched my mother go into the ground. If love is more than a desperate remedy for loneliness, I don't know what it is. What Fire Briskly Burning thought of love — what she thought of me — I never found out.

We had come to Utah Lake to see the

misery of Indians, and we saw it. So did people back east when Jackson sent prints there, made from the few negatives he managed to take back to Omaha. But they did no good. Oh, a deputation of Quakers descended on Grant, and a horde of missionaries descended on the Indians. But Sherman, Sheridan, and Custer were hell-bent on converting the entire race of Indians into dead redskins. The Indians believed they inhabited an endless ribbon of time. Ten thousand years on the Great Plains had done nothing to disabuse them. It took us whites just twenty-five years to show them they were wrong.

By March, I began to feel in my belly how starvation felt. I'd lie under the buffalo robes, stiff with cold — Fire Briskly Burning's furnace all but put out. I dreamed of the food I'd served the grandees on the hundredth meridian: roasted lamb and antelope, Chinese duck, oysters, buffalo tongue, braised bear in port wine sauce, washed down with champagne. After dinner, Durant had ordered a twenty-mile stretch of prairie grass set fire to entertain his guests. I wished to Christ I could feel its heat now; wished I'd some of the grass to feed the mules, one of which we'd slaughtered and dressed in the snow. I would eye the two remaining animals with avidity, but Jackson said we'd need them to climb out of the valley and over the Wasatch in the spring. He was thinking only of his goddamn camera and plates!

"If we're still here," I said gloomily from the depths of my beard, waterproofed with the bear grease used by the Indians to pomade their hair.

Jackson treated me to his most scornful look, and for once I returned it. In 1873, when Hayden invited him along as photographer on a survey of the Central Rockies, Jackson didn't ask me to accompany him. After Utah Lake, he considered me "pusillanimous." Seventy-three was the year the bison herds on the Central and Southern Plains had been all but killed off and, with them, the resistance of their rightful inhabitants, who'd been pushed by treaty and bayonet onto squalid reservations in Indian Territory. Seventy-three was also the year of the great panic, brought about by overspeculation, mostly in railroads, and the damn Germans' decision to stop minting talers, coins whose silver was mined in the American West. As a result, the Jay Cooke bank failed; Wall Street closed; work on the Northern Pacific transcontinental railroad halted; the country went onto the gold standard. The panic would finish Durant, who was like the rat that fell into a barrel of feed, gorged itself, and was exploded by its own appetite. Underneath the pile of prodigious events, I felt like a midget with a Barnum elephant on his back. And I felt as trapped by the snow as a grub in an Armour tin of spoiled meat.

"You should have stayed in Omaha and taken pretty pictures of the stiffs," said Jackson. Fed up with roughing it, I'd do just that, though it would be in Lincoln, not in Omaha, where I'd eventually set up shop. He dismissed me with a shrug and began to gnaw on a mule bone, his supply of apricots long since exhausted.

I remembered George Osler's saying, "They pay five dollars the ton for buffalo bones. They grind them up for fertilizer." I wondered what the going rate was for famished human bones.

We hadn't planned to spend the entire winter in the perishing cold. A fur trapper Jackson met in Denver told him of a Mormon settlement built around hot springs near the source of the Jordan River, to the north of us. But the snow lay too deep for the weakened mules, and Jackson refused to abandon his equipment and trudge there on foot. We tried, once, to reach the Jordan by traveling along the lake, but the poor mules slipped and slewed and slid onto their bellies like walruses.

I survived the long winter, but Fire Briskly Burning did not. Malnutrition and pneumonia took her, despite the bear grease in her hair. There is small nourishment in scanty fish and rodents. Her people took the body, its fire extinguished forever, and dealt with it according to their notion of the afterlife. I've asked myself many times what I'd have done if she had lived. I've never given myself a satisfactory answer. Jackson and I waited long enough for the mules to forage on the new shoots of grass, and then we walked out of the Wasatch and headed toward Omaha. We were silent while the wind in the pass told a complicated story of sadness and loss.

My spit never did freeze in midair, except in my imagination. I can't say I learned to read Indians, either. But I insist that I came to know one of them sufficiently to rid my mind of the prejudice that they were no better than dogs. Stranger yet, a Lakota chief would show me the future in my dreams. It would fill me like seawater does a sponge — or vinegar, for I'd choke on its bitterness.

Omaha, Nebraska, May 25 (Decoration Day) 1874

After my blue funk in the Utah Valley, I busied myself in the Jackson Brothers' studio, but William never again took me into his confidence or into the wilds with him to make pictures. My initiation into the mysteries of his art ceased, and I was left alone to hand-color the stereo views he sent back from the Rockies and the Yellowstone. I was only a little disappointed, for by now I'd realized I lacked his gift and would never have it, no matter how he might have led me — by insinuation or discipline — toward the sublime. The world was radiant for him, while I saw only glimmers in the general darkness, as you would on a sultry August night riven by an electrical storm: thrilling, terrible, and brief. For all my wanderings, I'm ordinary. I came to terms long ago with my littleness. A man is what he is — he can't rise so much as an inch above his shortcomings — Horatio Alger be damned! I don't hear you try to contradict me. I had my ages — childish, heroic, gilded, shameful — and I was content to let time stall around me, like a river shunted into a backwater. My atoms gloried in the change, as fish would to find themselves relieved of ceaseless effort. I languished, placidly, contentedly, thoughtlessly. At least I seldom gave my life a thought — me, who'd spent so much time examining it under the loupe of a fretful, helpless self-regard. I was worn-out from thinking, although what simmered below my mind's awareness of itself was as unknowable as the life of fish — be they in the canals of Mars or the muddy water of the Missouri. I mean to say that my mind kept its secrets hidden from me.

I've not much more to tell about my three years of idleness in Omaha, where I waited — my house scrubbed clean of remembrance, so to speak — to take up the thread of my life once more; and I will pass over them without further notice, except for a Decoration Day by the Missouri River. That was in 1874 — the year my history caught up with Custer's in the Black Hills.

That morning, I treated myself to steak and eggs at the hotel where Durant used to put up before the panic finished him; got shaved and had my long hair cut by the hotel barber; and then I walked out to the riverbank, intending to do some fishing. As a rule, I didn't care for fishing. Maybe I'd had my fill of God's fifth day of creation, having been shanghaied by circumstances into oystering as a boy. But I had given myself enthusiastically to the luxuries of the flesh at rest and knew there was nothing so restful as sitting on a flat stone, warmed by the sun, and diddling with a bamboo pole. I didn't much care what I caught with my godforsaken worm or even if I caught anything at all. I was glad to let my eye glaze over with the dancing river light and let my mind sink into its own tranquil ooze, sleepy with the murmur and drone of a hot May afternoon.

I must have fallen asleep and would have remained so had it not been for the ferocity of a chain pickerel that pulled the pole out of my hands and dragged it out onto the water. In a moment, it had bitten through the line and disappeared among the reeds and grass. I cursed the fish, for form's sake, though I didn't begrudge it the worm or the bamboo pole, either, even if it had cost me four bits. No, the pickerel had put an end to the last pretense of ambition for that holiday afternoon, and my thoughts turned toward a nocturnal visit to Madam Ida's. But as I was searching my mind for the girl I'd choose to light my firecracker, I surprised myself by flushing Chen out of one of memory's dark rooms. During the recent do-nothing years, I'd hardly thought of him at all — embarrassed, perhaps, by my indolence. Now, sitting on my flat stone,

I recalled how, years before on this same riverbank, Chen had chided me for a rage that had blown up in me as sudden as a squall. I don't remember now what had incensed me. Some highhandedness of the rich and powerful, I suppose. I had the soul of a muckraker in those days. Chen took my arm (a womanish gesture that made me flinch) and said, "You're too earnest, Stephen. Earnest men are sometimes good, like Lincoln; sometimes fanatical, like Booth. It's better to be calm; safer to take a tranquil view of things."

Chen wasn't perfect. I've idealized him in this recitation, but he had his faults, same as anybody — yellow, red, black, or white. While he was encouraging me to be philosophical about life, a man stepped out onto a pier just below us and dumped a litter of newborn pups into the river.

"What do you think of that?" I asked Chen, my anger flaring like a ribbon of magnesium once again. It may be common practice to drown unwanted cats and dogs at birth, but it's a cruel one, Jay.

"I have seen infant girls put into the river to drown," Chen said stoically.

I didn't like his attitude — and don't tell me human life is cheap in China, damn it! It's the same here. So maybe I tend to be self-righteous and too full of zeal. A man can't help what he is or doing what he must. Anyway, when I read in the paper how Custer was getting ready to march into the Black Hills, my days of idleness were at an end.

Fort Abraham Lincoln, Dakota Territory, July 1, 1874

When I first laid eye on General Custer, he was trimming his yellow mustache with the finicky attention of a French duke or an actor. I stood in the doorway, regarding his face in the ornate mirror he held in one hand while he snipped decisively with a silver scissors held in the other. He was considered handsome by many, but in my opinion a foppish vanity and fatuous self-satisfaction, darkened by cruelty and ambition, had made an otherwise ordinary face grotesque. Absorbed in his pruning, he didn't notice me at first, although he liked to boast that nothing escaped him. I began to worry that he'd suddenly look up and, provoked by being taken by surprise, wither me with his disdain. I'd read enough newspaper accounts of the famous Custer temper to fear his annoyance. Nervous as a weather vane, I was deliberating whether I ought to sneak out of the room, when he discovered me in the little gilded mirror. He caught my eye, and I caught his: We were bound, momentarily, by a single look of mutual fascination — mine tempered by fear, his black with suspicion. I coughed, and the spell broke. He laid the mirror down on his dressing table and turned to me.

"Who in the hell are you?"

"General Custer . . ." I began to stammer.

"*I* am General Custer, and I've never doubted the fact."

He didn't need to complete his asservation. His unspoken words hung in the cloying air of the room, whose walls shone with afternoon sun, as if with the reflected glory of the general's golden hair, dressed with cinnamon-scented oil: ". . . of my special destiny and greatness, you pint-sized worm."

I am on the short side — you can see that plainly enough — but I resented being thought of as a worm.

"I'm Stephen Moran," I said, this time without hesitation. "I'd appreciate the honor of accompanying you as expedition photographer. There's nothing I'd rather do, sir."

Of all the people I've known, Custer was the least bothered by modesty. He gave himself license to do or say anything that would enlarge his reputation, which he nourished with the care and single-mindedness of a horticulturist intent on producing a gaudier flower. Luckily for me, the general was not camera shy. During the war, he'd gotten himself photographed more often than anybody else in the United States, not excepting Lincoln and Grant. He stared at me awhile, ruminating over my proposition. To be always within range of a camera must have appealed to him.

"Have you ever taken pictures in the wilderness?" he asked. "Or are you one of those parlor snakes who take pictures of ladies and gentlemen posed grandly with a pot of ferns?"

I recounted my experiences at Bear River, in the Wasatch, and on the shore of Utah Lake. I omitted my pusillanimity. They appeared to satisfy him, although he continued to assess my meager frame skeptically. It was then I shrugged the saddlebag from off my shoulder so that he could see my medal. I had decided to wear it in order to trump any objections the general might raise concerning my fitness.

"Come closer," he said. "Where'd you get that? You didn't steal it, did you?"

"No, sir. I got it for heroism at Five Forks."

"Moran . . ." he said, shutting his eyes as if to find my history recorded in a dark corner of his mind. "Are you the bugle boy who rode to Springfield on the Lincoln Special?"

"I am, sir."

He opened his eyes and their light fell on me like a royal pardon.

I'd have congratulated myself on my cunning had I not already discovered in my twenty-five years how easily a megalomaniac could be manipulated.

"Then you're no parlor snake!" he shouted, slapping his thighs as though he meant to break into a gallop and, mounted on a four-legged stool, ride against all such perfidious men who might, if allowed to flourish, practice their oily seductions on his beloved and desirable wife, Libbie.

He twisted one end of his dandified mustache between his fingertips and broke into an uproarious laugh, which went on far longer than one would expect of a sane man.

I didn't know whether to guffaw fraternally, applaud his impersonation of a philandering reptile, or look down at my boots in embarrassment. I decided on the last.

His suspicions must have reared again, because he spoke my name sharply:

"Moran!"

"Yes, sir?" I said, snapping to attention. I offered him my abjection like a bribe.

"Why do you want to go with Custer into the Black Hills?"

His eyes glittered, and I saw the childish look of a naughty boy who plots the downfall of a burrow of gophers.

"To be at the center of the world."

The wattage of his gaze increased, a signal that I was to continue.

"General Custer is the hinge and pivot of great events, and where the general is, I want to be also. For a photographer, there's no better vantage from which to view the nation's most important era."

Growing expansive, Custer stretched his buckskin-clad legs, threw his head back, and shook out his golden curls.

"Moran, Custer prides himself on his knowledge of men and his judge of character. And he has made up his mind about you. And when Custer makes up his mind, nothing in heaven or on earth can change it. Do you know why that is?"

"No, sir, I don't."

"Because of his unswerving and unshakable belief in himself."

"What's in the general's mind concerning me?" I asked.

"You are a man fitted by experience and temperament to photograph Custer when he seizes the Black Hills in the name of the United States of America."

"I'm grateful to him — and to you, too, General."

"Not at all."

He waggled the fingers of his right hand at me like a king dismissing a retainer. I withdrew from his august presence.

Did I know at Fort Lincoln that I would kill Custer? It's hard to explain otherwise why I sought him out on the frontier and cajoled him with every ounce of guile my baffled heart could summon to take me with him into the last Indian stronghold on the continent. I wasn't brave, and I had nothing to prove, either to him or to myself. True, I didn't have what you would call prospects, but I wouldn't have risked life and limb in the Black Hills to improve my situation — no, not even for photography, however much I was infatuated with the notion that the world could be subjugated by a wooden box fitted with a lens. Custer had become, for me — rightly or wrongly — a shiny emblem pinned over a national disease that had taken the Indian ponies and buffalo, as well as Little Will, Chen, Fire Briskly Burning, a soused, derelict Indian in Omaha —

even my own mother. I suppose you think my mind was unbalanced, Jay; and maybe you'd be right. How could it have been otherwise?

The Black Hills Expedition, July 2–August 30, 1874

The following day, Custer and his 7th Cavalry, along with a hundred wagons, three Gatling guns, and a sixteen-piece band, left Fort Abraham Lincoln for the Black Hills, the holiest place on earth to the Lakota Sioux. They went in search of gold to ease the national crisis aggravated by drought, yellow fever, and a plague of locusts that could eat the clothes off a body and strip the fields of crops and the houses of their paint. The Black Hills belonged to the Lakota, given to them and their posterity by the Fort Laramie Treaty of 1868. White men were forever barred from them. None cared so long as the darkly forested and stony hills were judged worthless for farming or grazing cattle. But treaty be damned! We had a right to the land by virtue of our need. The panic had worsened, money had lost its value, businesses had failed, factories had shut their doors, and foreclosures were driving folks to the wall or — for those who could stake themselves to the means of emigration — to the West. Some of them had an inkling there were riches in Dakota's Black Hills: minerals, timber, maybe gold. They hoped for gold.

Look, if your only escape from a grizzly bear is to jump into a canoe and push out onto the water, you don't worry whose it is. And if the canoe's rightful owner tries to stop you, you kill him. That's what most people believe. More than likely, Jay, you do, too. And if I hadn't wintered with the Ute, I'd probably believe the same.

Two weeks later, we crossed the border into Montana and turned south. The next day, we entered Wyoming Territory. We followed the Belle Fourche River into southwestern Dakota and then skirted the north side of the Black Hills. I remember summer meadows brilliant with wildflowers. The men decorated their horses' bridles, laughing gaily like cavaliers on a picnic. Custer wore yellow monkey flowers in his long golden hair. At the Belle Fourche, I photographed him in his tent. He was writing accounts of the expedition for various newspapers and magazines and wanted a "thoughtful" picture to accompany his stories when he sent them east.

"Moran, we have discovered a rich and beautiful country," he said, stabbing the inkwell with his pen — a gesture made to illustrate what he meant to do with the country's inhabitants. (To tell Custer that the Black Hills had already been discovered by the Lakota would have been the same as a Roman slave's insisting, "I'm sorry, Caesar, but you haven't discovered Gaul; you've only stolen it.")

I bit my tongue and waited. Was it for this that Spotswood had told me to wait? To kill Custer? I'd made up my mind to finish him off, before there was not a bison left anywhere in America, except for those that would be herded into cattle cars and sent east to Buffalo Bill's Wild West show. To be honest — a nearly impossible virtue for human beings, no matter if they wear a sheriff's star or a parson's collar — the slaughter of the buffalo and the nine hundred Indian ponies on the bank of the Washita River infuriated me more than the reduction of the Indians. I suppose my sympathies are not uncommon even in the present age, when a brute will sometimes weep over a dead dog.

At the end of July, we stopped at French Creek, after a three-hundred-and-thirty-mile plod from Fort Lincoln, along what the Sioux called "Thieves' Road" — after Custer, whom Red Cloud had named "the

Thief." On the first of August, the mining engineers found a gold band thirty miles wide that the general might give to posterity, like a wedding ring. The expedition would alchemize the once worthless Black Hills. Speculators and prospectors, store- and saloonkeepers, gamblers and whores, claim jumpers and road agents would pile in, insisting that the "Indian dogs in our manger" be swept aside.

The general wanted his discovery commemorated, and I obliged with a photograph of him handing a message to Charley Reynolds, his chief scout, who carried the news to Fort Laramie. From there, it lit out by telegraph to the states back east and to the papers. Custer would glory, bask, and wallow in his fame for the rest of his life, which was, thankfully, short.

By winter, fifteen thousand emigrants had already arrived in the Black Hills — too many for the army to oust or for the Indians to kill. In the spring, Red Cloud and other of the Lakota's most illustrious chiefs went to Washington to protest against the incursion into their most hallowed ground. They were feted by their Great White Father; they ate off china plates. They were shown the city — even treated to an artillery salute, intended, perhaps, as a demonstration of

American military strength. Their entreaties were ignored. Red Cloud and the others returned to the Sioux Reservation, their hope of gaining the president's sympathy now a forlorn one. Grant issued an executive order to clean out the Black Hills of "hostiles." It would be open season on the last buffalo herds. After this piece of treachery, I didn't much care for Grant. I considered sending him my medal once again, but something told me I'd have need of it.

"Moran, I want you to take a picture of me at the summit of Harney Peak."

"A fine idea, General."

"I want it to insinuate in the minds of all who see it that at Custer's feet lie the immense riches of a new world. For that is what it is, Moran. A new and glorious world."

"I can do that, sir. I'll take it with the sun shining on the land, as if God Almighty Himself were sanctifying it for the United States!"

"So long as the light also shines on me."

Increasingly in my presence, he would drop the affectation of referring to himself as "Custer" — most likely because he ceased to regard me as someone apart from himself. I was absorbed into the Custer persona; he expropriated me just as he intended to steal — by force of eminent domain — the Black Hills from the Indians. Or maybe I was no more than a camera operated by his own inordinate egotism.

"Naturally, General."

I'd also make a glass plate of the summit undefiled by Custer's presence and would later send it to Walt Whitman.

William Jackson once said that photography makes ghosts of the world and that each picture shrinks the subject. He wasn't talking about its representation — not entirely; he meant that the subject matter itself grew smaller each time it was photographed. A mountain was diminished by every exposure. After a while, it would have no more substance than cottonwood lint or ideas in the mind of somebody who didn't much care to use it. If you took enough pictures of the West, the West would disappear. People would prefer to see life through their stereopticons. At the time, I didn't have the faintest idea what he was talking about; but after having taken so many pictures for so many years, I've come to understand him. I regret having allowed myself, through funk and faintheartedness, to shrink before his eyes during that famishing winter when I spent nearly all my life's allotment of love.

Known by the Lakota Sioux as Six Grandfathers (the place where Black Elk had his vision of the still point of the turning world), Harney Peak was named for General William S. Harney, hero of the Battle of Ash Hollow, waged against the Sioux, who called him "Woman Killer." It was renamed Mount Rushmore to honor a New York City pettifogger during a pleasure excursion in 1885. By then, Crazy Horse had been killed, and Red Cloud was an old man living on a reservation, impoverished and forgotten. On Harney Peak, the gigantic likenesses of Washington, Jefferson, Lincoln, and Teddy Roosevelt will one day be carved in granite. The idea that the head of Red Cloud — the great Lakota war chief who signed the Treaty of 1868 to preserve the land and bison for his people — should be included among them will be rejected.

Red Cloud said, "God placed these hills here for my wealth."

Custer said, "One day this land will be worth so much, you won't be able to buy its dust."

Sitting Bull said, "I won't sell even so much of my land as the dust."

Crazy Horse said, "One does not sell the land on which the people walk."

Crazy Horse appeared to me many times during the year when I thought my head would break open like an egg and my addled brain slip out onto the pillow, damp from fever dreams. That was the year I was nearly driven insane by terrifying premonitions.

Black Elk said, "I saw that the sacred hoop of my people was one of many hoops that made one circle, wide as daylight and as starlight, and in the center grew one mighty flowering tree to shelter all the children of one mother and one father. And I saw that it was holy."

Red Cloud said, "The white men made us many promises, more than I can remember. But they kept one: They promised to take our land, and they took it."

I'd promised myself that I would put an end to Custer, but it's hard to kill a man in cold blood. Especially a man I found — in spite of myself — fascinating. My perfect hatred for him was spoiled by a particle of envy. There was something of Lincoln in my makeup — if you'll forgive my presumptuousness — and also something of Custer. Later on, Crazy Horse would muddle me even more. I would kill the general, but I'd have to work myself up to it.

George Armstrong Custer was another American meteor: a man fated to burn brightly, only to be extinguished in the cold sea of time and forgetfulness. The forgetfulness reserved for legendary men and women, whose true characters — good or bad — lie buried beneath the sediment of stories told about them. Red Cloud, Sitting Bull, and Crazy Horse were also destined for oblivion, and even Lincoln is obscured by the thickets of myth that have grown up around him. Unlike them, however, Custer contrived his own deification. He campaigned against the forces of anonymity that overwhelm all but the most illustrious or infamous of our kind. He exaggerated his virtues and colored his vices, both of which were centered on a morbid courage. He risked his life and, unpardonably, the lives of men under his command. He wrote dispatches to the newspapers and the illustrated weeklies of the day concerning his exploits in order to locate himself at the center of stirring events. The Indians abominated him. Many whites despised him, but I suspect that most admired his dash and recklessness. More than any other man I can name, Custer was the stamp and image of Manifest Destiny and the perfect type of western man: heroic, lawless, and undisciplined.

After the expedition's triumphant return to Fort Lincoln, Custer stayed at the fort with Libbie, while Sitting Bull and Crazy Horse began to gather defiant bands of Cheyenne and Sioux up in the Powder River Country of Wyoming Territory, between the Bighorn Mountains and the Black Hills. I continued, in effect, as Custer's personal photographer, recording moments, both public and private, for the history that would one day open its bloody maw to receive him. At his request — a Custer request was a command impossible to refuse — I produced a series of prints for the Centennial Exposition at Philadelphia: the general with Bloody Knife, his favorite Indian scout; with the Custers' pack of eighty dogs; with his junior officers, planning the destruction of the Lakota Sioux; with Libbie in the parlor of their private quarters at the fort; and the general striking a pose that would become as recognizable as Napoléon's: arms folded across his chest, looking forward and slightly upward at his magnificent destiny.

At the end of March 1876, Custer was summoned to Washington to testify at proceedings brought against Secretary of

War Belknap, accused of enriching himself by the unlawful sale of civilian contracts at western forts.

"Moran, I want you to go east with me," he said while I immortalized him lacing up his cavalry boots. "Heads are going to roll in Washington, Moran, and Custer needs to be seen with his hand on the lever of the guillotine."

"Naturally, General."

I hadn't been east since '65, and the thought of visiting there pleased me.

"Be sure to take the stereo camera," he said. "My pictures are in great demand ever since I discovered gold."

"Excellent idea, General!"

"Libbie's grateful to you, Moran, for sharing your royalties with her. She's spruced our quarters with new curtains and furniture. Did I ever tell you that the writing table she's so partial to is the very same one where Lee signed the articles of surrender at Appomattox Court House?"

"No, sir."

I'd heard it often but pretended otherwise. I needed to stay on his good side if I was to get close enough to kill him.

"Sheridan gave it to me at the McClean house — a gift for Libbie. He doted on her."

The Civil War began in Wilmer McClean's

front yard in Manassas and ended in the parlor of his house in Appomattox, where he'd moved his family to escape the strife. There is a thread to tie together the most divergent events or the most unlikely persons, if one can find it.

We rode to Washington on the transcontinental railroad. My apparatus was packed in the baggage car. When we arrived at the Baltimore & Ohio Depot, where I'd set out with the body of Mr. Lincoln eleven years before, Custer waited inside the car until I could arrange the camera, prepare a negative, and take his picture as he descended onto the platform. I never saw a bigger ass than George Armstrong Custer! That morning in Washington, you might have thought it was Jesus arriving in Jerusalem on the back of a donkey, so laden with a tragic nobility did he appear. While we attended the impeachment hearings, I photographed him in his fancy regimentals, with a hand on the Holy Bible, swearing to tell the truth — a feat for someone used to embroidery; on the Capitol steps; outside Mary Surratt's boardinghouse and in the Arsenal courtyard, where she was hanged; by the Potomac, ready to throw a silver dollar across it — he'd have chopped down a cherry tree if he'd had a hatchet — and in a number of other poignant tableaux.

One picture I didn't take was of Custer knocking at the White House door; Grant refused to let him inside. He was furious with Custer for having implicated his brother Orvil in the trading-post scandal and, on the twenty-first of April, relieved him of his command. Happily, it was restored in time for the Little Bighorn. Later on, Orvil was committed to an insane asylum in New Jersey for a "monomania for large speculations."

"Moran," said Custer while we stood at the hotel bar drinking lemonade. He had taken the pledge in '61, after a disgraceful exhibition in front of his sweetheart, Libbie, and her starched father.

"Yes, General?"

"I want to go to Philadelphia to see the exposition."

"What about the Sioux War?" I asked.

"The Sioux will await Custer's pleasure. I want to see my pictures."

Camden, New Jersey, April 22, 1876

While Custer was admiring himself in Philadelphia, I crossed the Delaware on the Camden ferry and visited Whitman. A grievous stroke suffered three years earlier had obliged him to leave Washington and move into his brother George's Camden house. When George showed me into the front room, I found Whitman slumped on a sofa, scratching at foolscap with a pen. I thought he must be composing new verses for his *Leaves,* but on closer inspection, I saw what appeared to be a genealogy, perhaps the Whitman family tree. We had believed his book, like the poet himself, to be unstoppable; that even in death, he would manage to enlarge it with editions as natural as the rings marking a tree's annual increase. But now he was done with it and looked like a man preparing to give up the ghost. His rude health and rough manner had deserted him. He was worn-out, like the nap of a corduroy suit. I saw the bones of his winter and — when he lifted his gaunt face to mine — the remnant light that time conspired to quench. I thought then that he must be a great soul, however much his imperfections kept him human.

"I'm Stephen Moran," I said, since he didn't recognize in me the boy he had consoled in the Armory Square Hospital. I thought my name would be sufficient to bring to mind the author of the western photographs I'd been sending him ever since Bear River City.

"Stephen Moran . . ." he repeated in

bewilderment.

I hunted the room with my eyes; saw an oil painted by his friend, the Philadelphia artist Thomas Eakins, and on the wall, above a fernery, a photograph of William Henry Jackson that I'd taken in the Wasatch Range, after our winter sojourn with the Ute.

"I took this picture," I said. "Six years ago, in northern Utah."

"Ah! Now I recall the name. It's a fine photograph, Mr. Moran. I've admired the others you've kindly sent to me. I took inspiration from them."

"Do you know why I sent them?"

His bemused look grieved me, for it spoke of the slippage of a great mind toward its end.

"I was the bugle boy you recommended for Mr. Lincoln's funeral train. I played taps on the trip to Springfield. I've always been grateful for the notice you paid me."

I didn't mention the first time I saw him, by Sheepshead Bay. He might not have cared to be reminded of his vanished virility.

"There were so many young men. Though it seems to me I do remember your face — because of the eye patch, though I don't recall the circumstances. What brings you east, friend? If I were lucky enough to be a man at large in the West, nothing short of dynamite could relocate me."

I told him that Custer had taken me on as his photographer and that we'd come east to see the exposition. (I didn't mention the general's disgrace.) Whitman said he hoped he'd feel up to scratch enough to go. He was keen on Machinery Hall. He believed that machines would be the motive power to push the democracy forward into the twentieth century. He planned on going to Philadelphia with Eakins, if his strength didn't desert him entirely. He wanted to ride the Camden ferry once again. Looking at his hand, wondering, perhaps, what had become of its power to snatch from the air his mind's effusions, he recited, "What exhilaration, change, people, business by day. What soothing, silent, wondrous hours, at night, crossing on the boat, most all to myself — pacing the deck, alone, forward or aft. What communion with the waters, the air . . . — the sky and stars, that speak no word."

In my mind's eye, I saw him on deck, wearing his suit of iron gray, loosely cut and old-fashioned. The Good Gray Poet, "taken by strangers for some great mechanic, or stevedore, or seaman, or grand labourer" —

sadly, now, no more.

"Custer is a magnificent specimen of the American man," Whitman said later while we were drinking tea in the sunny kitchen. "You won't catch the general sipping horse piss like this."

"The general's teetotal," I said.

"Is he?" This news seemed shocking to Whitman, as if I'd told him Custer liked to dress up in Libbie's undergarments. "I would never have thought it. Grant's a man's man, though! Nothing but whiskey and cigars for him!"

Both manly vices would prove fatal when Death came for him — destitute and forgotten — in 1885.

"Custer will deal with the Indians," said Whitman, who must have forgotten his verses in praise of them.

"Yes," I said, to be agreeable. And I will deal with Custer, I thought.

"What do you think of love, Stephen?"

"Pardon me?" I said, much surprised by this question, which was apropos of nothing.

"Lately, I've been thinking a good deal about love," he said with a distracted air that made him look like a moon calf. "I thought I understood it, but now, now I'm not so sure."

Strange, isn't it, Jay, that the nearest I had gotten so far to an understanding of love was with an Indian girl who didn't speak English?

"It's a mysterious force to make men and women behave in the most extraordinary way."

Yes, I said to myself, not feeling qualified to interrogate the matter with him.

"You know, when I was a boy of five, General Lafayette picked me up from a crowded sidewalk and carried me down the street during his visit to New York. I have always believed that happenstance conjunction determined my destiny."

He lapsed into a silence fretted by wonder and regret while he played absently with his teaspoon.

"It cannot stand!" he said with sudden vigor. "My dismissal! To have been let go with such contempt; to be dismissed for having written a book 'full of indecent passages.' He called me 'a very bad man,' you know, a 'free lover.' No, I can't allow Harlan's calumny to go unanswered."

I knew that Harlan, secretary of the interior during Johnson's presidency, had sacked Whitman because of *Leaves of Grass,* which he judged obscene. That was nearly eleven years ago, and it had returned, the cheap denigration of his life's work and life, both: a grievance the old man gnawed, like a marrow bone, in his winter, his sad decrepitude. If he'd ever forgotten the affront. I could not pity him: I was no one to pity a great man, however reduced by age and sickness. I was sorry. We can feel sorry for people fallen on hard times without demeaning them by pity. Though I could have cried to see Whitman's rheumy eyes, his gnarled, arthritic hands, the remains of a coddled egg left from breakfast on his shirt. His great head waggled a little, the way an old man's will.

I stood and shook his hand. From his chair, he threw an arm around my neck and drew my face down to his and kissed me. Our beards entangled as briefly as our two lives had done — in Brooklyn, Washington, and now in Camden — and then they disentangled, one from the other, although he'd be often in my thoughts.

"Thank you for your visit, young man. Will you be stopping at the exposition?"

"Briefly, Mr. Whitman."

"Walt — call me Walt, as you would a comrade."

"Walt."

He smiled, and I watched his face undergo a metamorphosis that would have entranced

Ovid: It passed from the unalloyed joy of an elk at the summit of its range to the anguish of a deer, an arrow through its lungs and heart.

"Perhaps, I'll be able to visit it next month. Sadly, the organizers did not invite me to read my poems."

He would visit the Centennial Exposition and slide his fifty cents through the ticket window, like any ordinary citizen of the democracy he cherished and sometimes wrongheadedly defended. Still, you couldn't help but love him — at least I couldn't, who had heard him bellow his love while the waves crumbled on Brooklyn's pleasant shore when I was nearly twelve.

I left him sitting in the kitchen, upright in his chair, his saucer flooded with tea, without a backward glance — knowing that the door to my childhood, which I believed long ago dead and buried, had finally closed with the shutting of the Whitmans' front door on Stevens Street.

That evening, I crossed the Delaware to Philadelphia and joined Custer at the exposition. Two months later, a telegram from Salt Lake City would arrive there, electrifying visitors with the news that Custer and all his men (save one) had fallen at the Little Bighorn. Shortly afterward,

Whitman would write "A Death-Sonnet for Custer" and publish it in the *New York Daily Tribune.*

I.

From far Montana's cañons,
Lands of the wild ravine, the dusky Sioux, the lonesome stretch, the silence,
Haply, to-day, a mournful wail — haply, a trumpet note for heroes.

II.

The battle-bulletin,
The Indian ambuscade — the slaughter and environment
The cavalry companies fighting to the last — in sternest, coolest, heroism.
The fall of Custer, and all his officers and men.

III.

Continues yet the old, old legend of our race!
The loftiest of life upheld by death!
The ancient banner perfectly maintained!
(O lesson opportune — O how I welcome thee!)

As, sitting in dark days,
Lone, sulky, through the time's thick murk

looking in vain for light, for hope,
From unsuspected parts, a fierce and momentary proof,
(The sun there at the center, though concealed,
Electric life forever at the center,)
Breaks forth, a lightning flash.

IV.

Thou of sunny, flowing hair, in battle,
I erewhile saw, with erect head, pressing ever in front, bearing a bright sword in thy hand,
Now ending well the splendid fever of thy deeds,
(I bring no dirge for it or thee — I bring a glad, triumphal sonnet;)
There in the far northwest, in struggle, charge, and saber-smite,
Desperate and glorious — aye, in defeat most desperate, most glorious,
After thy many battles, in which, never yielding up a gun or a color,
Leaving behind thee a memory sweet to soldiers,
Thou yieldest up thyself.

I wasn't taken in by that horseshit, either.

San Francisco, May 10–16, 1876

If I'd ever been tempted to unknot the rope that bound my destiny to Custer's, it was during the six days I spent in San Francisco, while, confined at Fort Snelling, in Minnesota, the general wrangled, wept, and sulked in disgrace for having defamed brother officers — not to mention Orvil Grant — at the impeachment of the secretary of war. I was ravished by the city on the bay and by a woman living there.

Anna McGinn owned a studio on Kearny Street — a rarity at a time when photography was practiced mostly by men, if for no other reason than the weight and cumbersomeness of the apparatus, glass plates, and chemicals. Anna was making ambrotypes, an innovation superior to daguerreotypes but considered quaint by wet-glass snobs because they could not be reproduced on paper. They were suitable to hang on parlor walls or to enclose in little gold shrines for gents to carry in their coat pockets, like a cigarette case or a whiskey flask. But though she held me captive for a handful of spring days — never mind the San Francisco damp — I'd come to believe in my inalienable destiny as an assassin.

Nevertheless, those days do deserve mention as the pinnacle of my experience of love. Had I met Anna before my visit to Whitman, I could have told him what I thought of that most disquieting emotion. I said nothing about Fire Briskly Burning. He might have understood my feelings for her — he understood far stranger affections; but I wasn't sure if his racial tolerance was sincere or merely literary. Now that I think of it, I wonder whether I did love my winter squaw. She seems at this remove in time and space no more than a dream. If life is nothing but a swamp in which we lose our way, the affections are quicksand in which we drown.

I met Anna in a gaudy saloon on the Barbary Coast, Frisco's brawling, disreputable district, where every manner of vice and meanness could be found. She was there to deliver an ambrotype she'd made of a chanteuse for a miner whose pockets were lined with silver from the Comstock Lode. I was there to soak up local color and the rum brought by ship from the East Indies. I noticed her immediately; she had a striking profile, framed by hair that seemed in the light of the saloon's gas brackets to flash with emeralds. In the sunlight, her hair was ash-blond. She was small-boned and delicate — shorter than I, who had drunk enough rum to surmount a habitual timidity before the opposite sex. I noticed that her fingers were blackened by the silver nitrate of her trade, or "black art," as it was often called. I sidled down the bar and listened to her harangue the goggle-eyed miner, whose fickle affections had gone elsewhere. Anna got her money, and when she left the saloon, I followed her along Pacific Street to her studio on Kearny.

"I take pictures, too," I said — idiotically in retrospect. I stood in the middle of her studio, trying my level best not to sway or breathe.

"You stink of rum," she said, not deceived by my pantomime of sobriety.

"I took a drop against the damp. At the saloon up on Pacific. I noticed your fingers."

"What about them?" she snapped, loudly enough to upset my precarious equilibrium.

"They're stained black. So I knew."

"What do you want with me?"

"To make your acquaintance."

In answer to my smile, she raised her head defiantly; her green eyes glared. In a moment, I'd be showed the door, if not kicked and shoved through it. For a small package, she was fierce. I thought momentarily of Amazons and female mountain lions and wondered if I shouldn't sneak sheepishly out the door while I still had the power of locomotion. But the woman fascinated me for a reason I couldn't have explained at the time, even to myself.

"I'm in town on a visit," I said quickly, hoping to defuse an anger I could almost hear hiss. "I've been out west taking pictures."

She relaxed a little, and her eyes granted me a stay of judgment in which I might explain myself. I told her the story of my life, as much of it as I dared. She sat on a stool, her elbows on the counter, and listened attentively. I held the floor, as orators say. I held it well. I doubted if John Calhoun or Daniel Webster — or even Abraham Lincoln himself — could have done better. I was possessed of an eloquence I might have imbibed while keeping the dead man company, or else from the Barbados rum. When I'd had my say, Anna allowed that I might stay awhile. We talked about our work. She showed me several albums of her pictures — things she'd done for her own pleasure. I recall the portrait of a sockeye, caught in the Columbia River, she'd bought at Paladini's on the wharf. I had never in my life considered taking pictures of fish. Dead buffalo were more in my line, but she preferred small subjects, in consideration of the cramped studio.

She'd made a series of ambrotypes devoted to butterflies and moths — dead ones pinned to sumptuous fabrics: Japanese silk, Venetian cloth, Flemish lace, Italian brocade. They were gorgeous in their way. They would have delighted the eye and smoothed out the wrinkled brain of most people, but their prettiness rubbed me raw. Anna's photographs showed a side of the world contrary to what William Jackson had taught me to see: the stark and brutal reality of the western plains and the half-tragic, half-lunatic emigrants who crawled over them. If we knew what waited for us, would we alter our courses — or are we fixed hypnotically, like a compass needle on the lodestone of our destinies?

We kept company during the brief time allotted me by the urgency of history and my own death wish. We took our meals together and drank genteel spirits in keeping with the age's idea of decorum. Even in San Francisco, women could not stray too far from propriety without tripping over their petticoats into the abyss: Fashionable Van Ness Avenue is only a block from sordid Polk Street. We went to the music halls on Geary Boulevard; we walked along the bay and saw the distant ocean from the Presidio. Coming from Philadelphia, I'd had my camera and supplies taken off the train at Omaha and sent on to wait for me at Fort Lincoln. I wanted to see the city in the way ordinary people do: imperfectly and dreamily. I sometimes wonder if real life is more truly apprehended by eyes not pressed to the camera back — heresy to Jackson. To look through a camera can be like being made to stare at the sun.

Anna and I did not make love. I don't remember why. Maybe we didn't need to. She might have been afraid, although I doubt she was afraid of much. She'd been a midwife before she opened a studio; she'd held life in her hands, like a wire from a galvanic cell. Maybe death was too strong in me for an act so inspirited with life. Although I sometimes think that death is what gives lovemaking its desperate and terrible joy.

Did she sense my frostiness? No, that wasn't it: I was not — to my mind — the least cold toward her. As I recall, my mood was a match for the season and took its colors from the green of Golden Gate Park, with its vivid eucalyptus and pines. I've never been an optimist, but I was not cast down while Anna showed me her city. I was hardly aware of the dark purpose that had driven levity from my mind in Washington

City, in Philadelphia, and on the train when Custer and I were carried down the rails toward our fatal intersection. My happiness in being with Anna overruled, for a time, the murder in my heart. If you'll excuse the metaphor, she was a perfume drizzled over a corpse — man's or beast's, I'd had experience with both. No, there was nothing frosty in my attitude toward her; but she must have felt the sickness in me — in my soul, if you care for the word. The disease that undermined a perfect intimacy.

And yet she said to me, "Why don't you stay?"

"What, here in San Francisco?"

"We could open a studio together. Like your Jackson brothers."

I flirted with the idea while we took the Clay Street Hill Railroad up the steep way to Leavenworth — the city's first cable car. Two years later, Leland Stanford would build his up Powell Street to save his horses the brutal climb to Nob Hill, showing a laudable sympathy he never wasted on his Central Pacific coolies. Anna wanted me to admire the view of the port beyond the hill, with its Calvary of masts. I did admire it while my mind spun the thread of her notion into a tapestry in which I saw myself photographing the city and its hash of people. At the time, there was nothing like it for novelty and excitement. I thought I could get on well there with her.

"You can make all the outdoor views you like," she said as we stoked each other's fancy. "The city's growing like a field of Jimson weed. I'll keep on with my portrait work. There's plenty of business to keep us both busy. After a while, we can take a bigger studio and live on top of it."

"Might do," I said, my imagination electric with the prospect of a new start. I saw myself living fixed, in a comfortable room whose window looked out on a street instead of on scenery flying past a train's or else plodding by at the speed of a mule. I'd been on the move for fifteen years, ever since I boarded the *Marion* at Brooklyn, a green recruit. I felt played out, as if every mile of the thousands I'd covered had cost me a grain of sand or a particle of the iron a person is born with — call it courage or will, as you like. Suddenly, I felt I'd aged twice over during my twenty-seven years. I was tired of flight and of the black compulsions misdirecting my nagging heart. Who was Custer to me that I should forfeit the ordinary life of a man to destroy him? What was Fire Briskly Burning, or the Lakota Sioux, or the bison and ponies that I should spend unquiet days and restless nights contemplating their piteous ends?

We went into a tearoom near Lotta's Fountain and ate some fancy scones. The turmoil of my thoughts must have showed on my face; or perhaps Anna, like anyone used to looking hard, was able to see more clearly than most what my face concealed. I was expert at masking my fears and desires.

"What's wrong, Stephen?"

"Nothing. I'm thinking is all."

"The frontier's no place for you," she said gravely. "Out there is death to a sympathetic nature, to reason — to anything but what is violent and uncouth, selfish and absurd. You've seen enough of the Wild West for one lifetime, Stephen. Here, you can begin to mend."

"Am I broken?" I asked. I knew the answer already, but I was curious to hear her opinion of my . . . soul. Damn it, Jay, I'll use the word with or without your blessing! What were Crazy Horse's dreams if not the glass plate by which his soul was made visible? I could not ridicule the idea of a human soul and still believe in that Indian and his visions of the future. Which I do!

"From what I know of you, yes," she said softly. "I'm afraid of what will happen when you go back to your wilderness."

She knew me well enough, for I would go back. I knew it while I washed down the last sweet crumb of scone with the last bitter swallow of tea. The West was an enormous dynamo, and I felt its current pass through my body, aligning my atoms with its own. (Unless I mistook Death for the West. If Anna was right, they were identical.) Custer waited for me in Dakota Territory at Fort Lincoln; Crazy Horse waited for us both by the Little Bighorn.

A commotion outside brought me sharply back to Frisco. A horse had lain down in the street, upsetting a wagon overloaded with sheet iron. The driver was whipping the horse with an iron rod. The crowd that had gathered was divided as to whether he should refrain from or else continue his bloody reprisal. I wished George Osler had been among them with a shovel. I knew then that it didn't much matter where I happened to be: Everywhere was the same. You know what people are like.

She must have "read my light," for she shrank back a little and let the conversation die. She never again took up the idea of my staying in San Francisco. So perhaps she *was* afraid and felt it best to keep herself, finally, at a safe distance from me, like a healthy person does a house under quarantine.

After six days of dithering with my own manifest destiny and deluding myself with the pretty fiction of normality, Custer wired with news of his reinstatement. He was at Fort Lincoln, readying his men for the final assault on the Cheyenne, Sioux, and Arapaho gathered in their thousands by the Little Bighorn River, which the Indians called "Greasy Grass." I said good-bye to Anna at the depot without regret, eager to join Custer, whose attraction was stronger than love or whatever it was in me that had threatened to deflect my solemn purpose.

The Little Bighorn, Montana Territory, June 25, 1876

While Custer was kissing Libbie good-bye at Fort Lincoln, their avid lips never to join again in this world, Sitting Bull, transcendent war chief and holy man of the Lakota Sioux, was conjuring from the next world an ecstatic vision — conducted, like lightning down a lightning rod, by the sacred pole he danced around in rapture. He saw, he told his two thousand warriors, white men, upside down, riding against the rim of the sun. He saw them fall into the lap of the earth, which belonged to all people and also to animals. Sitting Bull said that in his vision — assembled from atoms of smoke and dream — the white men had no ears because they were deaf to reason and to the persuasions of the Great Spirit.

"It's through its mysterious power that we, too, have our being," Sitting Bull told his people, "and because of it we yield to our neighbors, even to our animal neighbors, the same right as ourselves to inhabit this vast land."

By this vision, Sitting Bull knew that his people were promised a great victory over the pony soldiers riding against them. He did not see and did not say, after dancing the Sun Dance in the Valley of the Rosebud, that in nine years he would ride a horse around the ring in Buffalo Bill's Wild West show, with Annie Oakley and a few mangy bison tamed by the white man's whip. Sitting Bull was of the Hunkpapa tribe, a Lakota word meaning "head of the circle." None can tell when he will trade his place at the top for one at the bottom. Just so, are we caught — all of us — in a desperate round, fixed and inescapable as the moon's orbit.

Do you believe in coincidence, Jay? If so, it's easy to dismiss the thread that winds through the life of Sitting Bull and Custer and so much else besides in this, my bewildered recollection of the time when America forged its iron union and annealed it in blood. I don't believe in it, but, rather, in the providential confluence of all things and beings who share a common earth.

Sitting Bull was as great a man as Lincoln; both were brought to earth by a bullet to the head.

We've come to the familiar part of my story, one that nearly everybody knows: the Battle of the Little Bighorn — Custer's Last Stand, or his "Last Fight," as it was known by millions who admired the commemorative lithograph distributed in '96 by Anheuser-Busch to taprooms and saloons from the East Coast to the West. It would bore me to go into it again, and you to hear it. What's more, I'm nervous and excited finally to have reached the climax of my story.

Suffice it to say, Custer believed he could destroy the Indians by surprise, just as he had done on the banks of the Washita in '68; and at noon, on the twenty-fifth of June, he prepared to attack the village — the biggest Custer's scouts had ever seen in thirty years of "Injun-fighting." A thousand lodges, two thousand warriors, and five thousand women, children, and old men of the Lakota Sioux, Cheyenne, and Arapaho tribes, along with renegades who'd jumped their squalid reservations — all crowded against the Little Bighorn River. After the general had divided the regiment into thirds and sent Major Reno's and Captain Benteen's columns elsewhere, his remaining battalion consisted of just two hundred and ten troopers unseasoned in frontier warfare and a photographer outfitted with a camera and a darkroom tent.

"Tomorrow, Moran, we'll be famous," Custer boasted from the saddle. "My heroism and your pictures of Custer with his boot on the throat of the enemy — famous!"

The fringes of his buckskins riffled in the breeze, and his yellow hair hung down in curls from under a wide-brimmed hat while Custer posed for my camera. I hadn't yet made up a plate — and never would for him again — but I pretended to take his picture. It would have been his last. Then he rode off, up Medicine Tail Coulee, toward the riverbank where Sitting Bull, Crazy Horse, Red Hawk, and an infuriated multitude waited — armed with hatchets, bows and arrows, coup sticks, and quirts, not only them, but also with new repeating rifles. In his fabulous egotism, Custer had left the Gatling guns and sabers on board the supply boat, the steamer *Far West,* moored on the Yellowstone. He thought he'd have no need of them. He thought that Custer would be enough. He believed in himself, which is the undoing of all who hope to climb to immortal fame over the dead bodies of inferiors. In his mind, the name Custer rhymed with Caesar.

The Indians took just as long as it takes a hungry man to eat a meal to overrun us. I was seized by an excitement unlike any I've ever known. It was unnatural. Ferocious. Inhuman. I threw away my camera, pulled a carbine from a dead soldier's stubborn grip, and rushed after the general, who was standing among a knot of panicked skirmishers, firing his six-guns at the war-whooping and -painted Indians flying past them on their ponies. Like a distracted devil, I screamed and pulled my hair — nearly insane with the thought that one of the braves would cut Custer down before I could reach him. I've always credited temporary insanity with my delivery from certain death that day: Indians respect and admire lunatics, believing them vessels of the unseen.

My resentment and simmering hatred for Custer had caught up with me and then jumped ahead, leaving me to scramble madly after it. The mountain of bones picked clean of flesh by his appetite and that of so very many others — animal and Indian bones, Chinese and Mexican bones — all at once they enjoined me with the peremptoriness of a holy commandment to vengeance. I was thirty yards from Custer — maybe forty, no more than that — when I saw a Cheyenne warrior take aim along the barrel of a Winchester. Custer was busy fending off a renegade's lance; he would have fallen from the Cheyenne's bullet. I sighted my carbine and fired — that's wrong: I didn't aim; I couldn't have done anything so deliberate in my besotted state of mind. I fired at the behest of a violent history. A man immersed in that history, it lent me its murderous instinct. I fired the rife without a thought and hit the general in the temple. By the time I'd clambered up the hill — Custer's, they call it now — its white defenders were dead. I grabbed a Springfield from one of them and sent a second bullet through the bastard's heart.

"God damn you to hell!" I screamed, but he was already out of range of my voice.

Two women came and broke Custer's eardrums with an awl because the words he had spoken to Chief Stone Forehead after the slaughter by the Washita — Custer's promise that he would never again make war on the Sioux — had run out of his ears like water, as if they had been sealed with wax.

An Arapaho warrior clubbed me with a stone hatchet, and I fell swiftly into oblivion. If I thought anything as I suffered Death to walk out from its vantage to take my pulse, it was that I would soon be parting with my scalp. But when I shrugged back into consciousness, it wasn't Death who loomed over me, but Crazy Horse, more fearsome than any Catholic harvester of souls. He was taking the measure of my heart with a gaze that seemed almost to heat my blood — to make it boil up like coffee in a pot left too long on the stove. He was the most extraordinary-looking man I ever laid eye on. I assert it not as an opinion but as a fact impossible to gainsay, because he would not allow his picture to be taken and none ever was, except once by — I almost said "accident," but I'm not sure that the universe allows accidents. If ever a man — white, red, black, or yellow — had the fat light seeping from his bones, it was Crazy Horse. He rode to battle in nothing but a breechcloth, so his bones were distinguishable underneath the lean and muscled flesh. I ought to have feared him; any other white man would have. But I didn't, even though he didn't look kindly at me. He stared at me as a naturalist would at a never-before-seen insect. I didn't squirm, much less whimper or beg for my life. My courage — it was hardly that, but let the word stand for what my behavior in his presence and during the battle resembled — my courage, then, and my having murdered Custer — they perplexed him.

"Why did you kill the Yellow Hair?" he asked. I suppose I must have been the most extraordinary white man he'd ever laid his two eyes on, in spite of my puniness.

"Because he killed too many to be permitted to live."

"Too many what?"

"Men. Soldiers. Indians. Women, children, old men. Buffalo. Black Kettle's nine-hundred ponies by the Washita. His dogs."

I spoke in the Lakota tongue, or he spoke in English, or we spoke together some sensual language known by animals or else in the mineral one of rocks — for the Indians believe even they are alive. God-damn it, Jay, I'm not Francis Parkman or even Ned Buntline! What happened to me by the Little Bighorn River was mystical as well as murderous. It's impossible to understand it in any prosaic way.

"Are you one of those white people who

wish to save Indians by bringing them the comforts of your Jesus?"

It was trick question, and I knew it. Instead of answering, I recited a line of Whitman's: "The red aborigines,/ Leaving natural breaths, sounds of rain and wind, calls as of birds and animals in the woods, syllabled to us for names,/ Okonee, Koosa, Ottawa, Monongahela, Sauk, Natchez, Chattahoochee, Kaqueta, Oronoco,/ Wabash, Miami, Saginaw, Chippewa, Oshkosh, Walla-Walla,/ Leaving such to the States they melt, they depart, charging the water and the land with names."

"Is that written in your Bible?"

"In *Leaves of Grass.*"

Crazy Horse nodded; he had already glimpsed the future and had seen there the end of his people's dominion over the Great Plains, at Wounded Knee, which would coincide with the end of Whitman's great poem.

"I have heard of this book," he said. He bent forward, lowering his face toward me; and for a moment, I thought he meant to kiss me, as Whitman had done in Camden, sensing in his humiliated body a coming night that might be other than mystical. Our two gazes entangled — Crazy Horse's with mine and mine with his. I descried intimations of a truth that I couldn't grasp.

Crazy Horse said, "Remember this moment well."

"I will," I said solemnly, like a godfather who has been entrusted with a childhood not his own.

"I'm going to spare your life so that you'll never be free of me."

It was then I began to be afraid.

CODA: CRAZY HORSE

How curious! how real!

— Walt Whitman,
Starting from Paumanok

Lincoln, Nebraska, 1901

I did three good things in my life: I killed Custer; I rescued a child, although it was too late to save her; and I refused to sell my photograph of Crazy Horse, even when I went bankrupt and lost the studio. I could have named my price. What wouldn't *The Atlantic Monthly, The New York Daily Tribune, Harper's Weekly,* or Whitman's old paper the *Brooklyn Daily Eagle* have paid for the only picture of Crazy Horse in existence? It would have made me rich — richer than most of the prospectors who went looking for gold and lost their shirts instead.

The wonder of it was how it came to be. My camera was lying in the tall grass, where I'd left it in my rush to scrabble up the hill and dispatch Yellow Hair to the corner of hell reserved for him since the Washita River campaign. The Indians never saw it, although it wasn't far from where Crazy Horse and I had searched each other's hearts or brains or whatever organ is capable of registering the minutest tremors of another's soul, which must be like the crystal in a radio or the lens of a telescope down which far-flung stars are borne. I've never been sure how the trick was accomplished that knotted our two minds together — not for eternity, which is only a fancy of theologians, sentimentalists, and wives, but for the year after Crazy Horse was killed at the Soldiers' Town on the White River. All during that year — I was going on thirty — I'd wake from sleep with a blinding headache, as if what I'd seen behind my closed eyelids — second sight — temporarily blacked out the daylight. That was in the late summer of 1877, when Crazy Horse ensnared me in his dreams of the future. I think he knew at the Little Bighorn that the summer of '77 would be his last — the curtain was ringing down forever on the ancient ways of his people, whom he and Sitting Bull had brought together for one final act of resistance by the magnetism of their stupendous wills.

I wore my medal during the Battle of the Little Bighorn. I hadn't put it on since my first meeting with Custer at Fort Lincoln, when I saw his self-satisfied face rising in the round moon of his hand mirror. But before we rode into the Powder River Country, I pinned it to my coat — at the bidding, I've always thought, of something that lies beyond the human mind and its weak influence on the world. Crazy Horse could have mistaken the tarnished scrap for a souvenir of the murder of his people and had the honor of cutting my throat. But instead, he looked at it gravely and then surprised me by asking if he could have it. I gave it to him and, in return, he gave me the medicine bundle from around his neck. Did these two talismans harmonize the vibrations of our separate hearts? You're a medical man, Jay. What do you say?

"What you're telling me, Stephen, has nothing to do with medicine or science."

What has it to do with, then?

"The occult — which I don't give a hang about. I'm surprised at you! I always took you for a sensible man."

Maybe it's the blood pressure. It's elevated. I saw it in your face this morning.

"It's too high, Stephen. I won't kid you. You're headed for another heart attack if you're not careful. You be sure to take the medicine I left."

I will, though I don't think it will do me any good. But you've been a good doc and a better friend to me, Jay.

"So tell me about Crazy Horse's picture."

After the Little Bighorn, I didn't return to Fort Lincoln. I was finished with the army, and, believing I had perished with Custer's battalion, the army was finished with me. I took my camera — left the tent, chemicals, and plates behind in the prairie grass — and walked all the way to Omaha. I stayed with Edward Jackson in the Jackson Brothers' portrait studio. I didn't take any pictures then, but I helped him and William's wife, Mollie, make hundreds of stereo cards of Mesa Verde and the Navaho for William Jackson, who was traveling with the Hayden Survey team in New Mexico at the time.

One day, while I was examining my camera to see if it'd been damaged in the fighting, I discovered an unbroken glass-plate negative inside. I almost threw it away. Once a wet plate dries, it's worthless; and any image that might have been laid down on the silver is gone. But something made me develop it. I realize it's beyond the realm of science and possibility, but the negative bore the image of Crazy Horse. It was as wonderful a find as the image of the dead Christ's face on the Shroud of Turin, seen for the first time since His crucifixion, when it was photographed three years ago. Who can say how His face was imprinted on that ancient rag? Who can say how — whether by happenstance or the mysterious workings of fate — the image of Crazy Horse came to be on my negative? Unless . . .

"Unless?"

The plate was exposed by the radiance of his bones — the fat light blooming from Crazy Horse at the moment of his ecstasy.

"You read too many books of the wrong kind. What's that you're reading now?"

From the Earth to the Moon.

"Jules Verne again! I tell you, Stephen, he'll drive you crazy with his fantastic notions. He's the worse kind of author for an impressionable mind like yours. A photograph of a dead Indian chief taken by his bones! Radio, isotopes — whatever do they mean?"

Words from the future, Jay, carried backward down the stream of time in Crazy Horse's dreams, like gold in a sluice — no, not gold, for his dreams were too ominous to be objects of desire; say, rather, that I picked them up from the gravel, like broken bits of shell. I almost knew their meaning.

Almost. Let's say I knew it the way a diviner knows hidden water by his rod: He feels it and — in his heart — knows it.

"I've never heard such lunacy!"

I've kept the secret of Crazy Horse's picture to myself for more than twenty years. I'm only safe in telling you now because, not long ago, I destroyed the plate.

"Why would you do such a thing?"

Are you laughing up your sleeve at me, Jay?

"Not at all! I've always admired you as a storyteller. Nobody can beat you and Mark Twain for exaggeration and invention. It's the only reason I've stayed your friend for as long as I have."

You don't believe a word of what I've been telling you.

"I wouldn't say that, Stephen. I'm sure you've told a few truths, only I'd need a rocker box to separate them from the gravel of outrageous fabrications. What possessed you to spoil the negative of that Indian, if it was worth so much?"

Something tells me I've come to the end of my thread. The thread that sewed my life in whipstitch to Whitman, Grant, Lincoln, Durant, Jackson, Custer, Crazy Horse. I swore to him — took an oath the last time he came to me in my sleep — never to let another person see his face. In his life, he had dreamed himself onto the other side of our world — the visible one, which he knew, in his wisdom, is only shadows. It was his great gift to sift from the illusory Phantoscope of images what is real. During the year of my headaches, he showed me it; and, what's more, he showed me the future from the vantage of the afterlife. He was a shaman, after all, and a most powerful personality — a seer, like Sitting Bull. Seers believe that the future already exists, and maybe they're right. How else do you explain prognostications and the glimpses of it that come to clairvoyants and oracles? Crazy Horse saw almost clear to the end, and so did I, although I recollect only a fraction of what he revealed to me in dreams — his dreams, which were like a lens trained on what will happen next . . . what's already happened on the other side, as though he'd been granted a fabulous and frightening look at an encyclopedia published centuries hence.

It was harrowing for me — that year of visions. I used to wear his medicine bundle to bed, afraid I'd disappear into the future or wake up insane or not wake up at all. I wish I'd never seen what lies waiting for us. Was it for this that Spotswood told me to wait?

But a vision cannot be refused or denied.

"What did you see that was so terrible, Stephen?"

I'll tell you what I remember. But first, I want to tell you about the Mexican girl I found outside Lamy. I was a mail clerk for the Santa Fe Railroad at the time. This was in 1879. I gave up the railroad — that is to say, I gave up the need to be in motion, which obsessed me my whole life — and opened the studio when I settled here in Lincoln in '82. I contented myself with making portraits of "stiffs," reading in no particular order books borrowed from the library, going to concerts and lectures on the Pygmies and the Hottentots, illustrated with magic lantern slides. It's a sickness in some people, a kind of extreme restlessness: the wish to be always moving. It must be what drives so many millions to pack up and go west. I was fed up with it. Ever read anything about such a disease in your medical books?

"Never. Seems a subject more in line with the authors you favor. Perhaps in the morbid imaginations of Poe or Hoffmann you might find such a notion. A dose of salts would have done them both good. And you, too."

I never put much stock in salt.

"If you're ribbing me about my shares in

Lincoln's salt wells, you needn't bother."

I don't mean to smile, Jay. . . .

"If you'd told me you were in contact with a fortune-teller, I wouldn't have taken a bath. Damn it, you remember the surveyor's report: 'There is no question of the vast wealth that will someday be derived from this region.' Lincoln salt was supposed to be finer and more plentiful than Syracuse's!"

Whiskey need refreshing?

"I won't say no. You shouldn't be drinking, Stephen. Not with your heart."

Just half a jigger.

"You've got the heart of a man twice your age."

That would make me a hundred and six. And more than likely dead.

"My point exactly. But I won't lecture you."

I've learned that the most determined hearts can be undone by a small thing. It might as well be a shot of bourbon as a bullet.

"Well, aren't you going to tell me about the Mexican kid?"

Sorry, I seemed to have jumped the track. In those days, it was my habit to explore the countryside whenever we were stopped for any length of time. So when the train put into Lamy — a fly speck on the map — to repair the boiler, I hired a mule and went out onto the desert to take pictures. You've never been in New Mexico, have you, Jay?

"I've never in my life been south of Kansas City."

The desert's worth seeing.

"So I've been told."

In the desert, there's a drought of water, and there's also a dearth of light when the sun is swallowed by piling clouds and the thorn trees, the cactus, the sedge grass are quenched. They appear to die the instant the light goes out of them, but although they wither, turning brown and brittle, they're only dormant, because they hold within themselves water and also light — maybe no more than a symbol's worth of both, but enough. And when the rain comes, the trees, bushes, and grass vivify; and when the dark clouds go, they shed their radiance once again. Jackson used to say that what the photograph can do better than the human eye or an artist's hand is to render the austerity of the world, which is the place to look for the world's purpose and meaning. And I've found no greater austerity than in the desert.

"The girl, Stephen."

I found her sitting by the body of a dead

Mexican. She was cried out and nearly dead herself with thirst. The man — he was her father — had been shot through the chest. His serape was stained with the rust of dried blood, and his big mustache was stiff with it. She looked to be four or five years old. I gave her water and a little food, and when she could speak, she told me two men had shot her father and taken his horse and saddlebag. My Spanish isn't the best, and when a spate of Mexican would bubble up from her, I couldn't follow. From what I was able to understand, her mother had died of fever the day before, and her father had been taking her to stay with an aunt. I couldn't discover where the aunt lived; I suppose the girl didn't know herself. I climbed to the top of a hill bristling with acacia, but I could see nothing except more desert. So I thought it was best to take the girl, whose name was Carmelita, back with me to Lamy.

"You couldn't very well have left her there."

The thought crossed my mind, like a drop of vinegar in milk or a fly on a cake. The brain can conceive of such horror, Jay!

" 'An imp of the perverse.' We're all prey to them."

I suppose so.

"What happened when you got to town?"

I left her at the mission church.

"A sensible thing to do."

And then, a little while later, while they were stoking the locomotive boiler, I went back for her.

"What in heaven's name for?"

I don't really know. Unless I was ashamed: They say the thought is father to the deed.

"What would you have done with a five-year-old Mexican?"

Taken care of her, I guess. I wasn't thinking. I put her to bed in the mail car, where I'd made a kind of parlor for myself, and waited for the train to go on to Albuquerque. By the time we arrived, I'd realized the impossibility of keeping her. I knew nothing about children. I knew nothing about Mexicans. I was living on a train.

"You were living in a dream."

When we got to Albuquerque, I left her with the sisters.

"Just as you should have. Drizzle a little water in my drink, will you?"

The next time we laid over in Albuquerque, I went to visit her at the mission. They told me she'd died of a fever not long after I'd left her there.

"More than likely, the same that took her mother. Yellow fever, malaria — there was nothing you could have done."

Crazy Horse said, "White men want acorns without the oak tree."

"I've got no time for mysticism, Stephen. Not Swedenborg's or even Emerson's, and certainly not a bloodthirsty Indian's."

You don't believe Crazy Horse came to me in my dreams?

"Frankly, no, but it's entertaining as all hell, though I do wish you'd hurry up and finish. You tell a story like a cancan dancer lifting up her skirts."

I remember how he stood and pointed into a distance that had no end or horizon but seemed to go on and on. My eyes — I had two of them in my dream — became tired and burned, and I would have closed them or looked elsewhere, but there was no turning away from it. Just as Jackson had done, Crazy Horse was teaching me how to see the world for what it is — for what it will be one day.

"God Almighty, Stephen! You should go on the stage."

I saw the Great Plains divided and subdivided by boundary lines, railroad lines, telegraph lines, and the lines of instruments not yet dreamed of. Paths trampled underfoot by Indians and bison, emigrants and their cattle became roads of gravel, macadam, asphalt, and concrete. The bison passed into history, and so did the ancient people of the Great Plains and of the continent — passed into folklore and ethnology, as curiosities and relics of an age when time and the land had yet to be apportioned. Other species of animal and vegetable life also were extinguished by poisons that dropped from the sky and rose up like dust from the earth and fell into the waters of the rivers and their tributaries, the lakes, and even of the sea, where great whales sang of their misery and oysters crowding the shorelines sickened and shriveled and all manner of fish and the life that gave them sustenance perished from the earth. I saw crops fail and the grass disappear from the prairies and the loam crumble to dust, and I saw the dust blown upward into a brown and turbid atmosphere, which darkened the Great Plains and the lungs of the people living there — coiling and uncoiling its atoms until even the cities of the East grew dark beneath the pall. And birds, whose delight it was to slip through the clear skies, like a needle through cambric, and at the end of the day to rest in the trees or in the tall grass, singing to our delight the canticles of plenty — one by one, they fell silent, the furnace glowing within each small breast put out. That was the final dust storm, when rock was scoured of soil by wind and the inexhaustible aquifers beneath it were emptied and the sweet noise of water became like the dry cough of seeds rattling in an empty gourd. The Great Plains now resembled the Sahara, and roofs and steeples sown thickly on the East Coast and on the West had vanished beneath dead oceans chilled by floes that, since the beginning of time, had been like shingles on the roof of the world — chilled and then warmed by the enraged sun, which reigned without softness or mercy over earth's toppled kingdoms.

Near the end of his dreaming in me, I saw how earth came to resemble its moon and the near planets, revolving to no purpose in its worn orbit until, at the end of time — for time will end — it fell into the sun.

"You picture a world —"

Crazy Horse pictured it.

"Crazy Horse, then, to humor you. A world without a morsel of goodness or hope and with not even so much as a tussock of grass to clutch and pull ourselves from the mire. It goes against the American grain!"

Jay, there are always optimists who will step close to a house on fire because they happen to be cold. They see good in everything — even the day when bees will be extinct, because they fear the pain of an occasional sting.

"What the world needs is more good whiskey to rid it of its rust. Here — doctor's orders. In your present frame of mind, a jigger won't do you any harm. Stephen, I never took you for a weakling. We'd still be sitting on Plymouth Rock if we'd been afraid of getting our hands and consciences dirty. I held my tongue while you smeared the good name of Custer, who was a great American in my book. Virtue is unattractive in a man and a nuisance in a woman. And where would we be without Durant and the railroad? On the other side of the Mississippi, cutting one another's throats for a piece of played-out land. I won't cry over the buffalo or the Indians. Neither did the country any good, so far as I can see. Thanks for the whiskey — I've got to be going. Bess'll scalp me if I'm late for Sunday dinner. I'll see myself out. Get some rest — you must be tired after so much jawing. And I wouldn't worry too much about the future if I were you. Like it says in the Bible, 'The earth abideth forever.' "

You cleared out of here as if you didn't want

to be saddled with a corpse before you could eat your roast. Not that I blame you; nobody does a piece of veal like your Bess. I've always envied you your life, Jay. I don't know what you made of my story. I suppose you've heard ravings from the sickbed just as outlandish.

The last time Crazy Horse came to me, he said, "I am destined to live forever in an empire of grass and wind and water, when all else is dust. There, fish thread their silver or their gold through sunlit rivers, birds fly their shadows over the hills, and apple, pear, and plum trees drop their fruit, unbruised, onto the tall grass, as if it were a gift left on the doorstep for our refreshment. At the end of the day, we lie down together in the lee of the hill and give thanks to all that is alive for what is alive in us — certain that the sun will rise again. I do not see you there."

He turned and walked away, leaving me to wonder if I'd heard him correctly or if he'd even spoken at all. And then I thought I saw my mother, Lincoln, Whitman, Sitting Bull, Fire Briskly Burning, Chen — all of them walking, nonchalant and beautiful, across the rim of the sun. And I seemed to hear drums and the distant thunder of many millions of buffalo galloping across tall prairie grass leaning in the wind.

How beautiful and perfect are
the animals! . . .
How perfect the earth, and the
minutest thing upon it!

— Walt Whitman,
"To Think of Time"

ACKNOWLEDGMENTS

This book would not have seen the light of day if not for the publisher and editorial director of Bellevue Literary Press, Erika Goldman, who not only recognized in it a story needing to be retold to a new generation of Americans but also saw in its first draft a weakness needing to be overcome. She has my admiration and thanks, as does her colleague and the press's founding publisher, Jerome Lowenstein, M.D., as well as its associate editor, Leslie Hodgkins; publishing assistant, Crystal Sikma; publicist, Molly Mikolowski; and production and design director, Joe Gannon. I write with an ideal reader in mind. For this book, there were two of them: Erika and Carol Edwards, who edited it.

I am indebted to Edward Renn and David Moore, whose friendship creates an interior space conducive to the task of writing. I am grateful for the examples of a conscientious and compassionate nature set by my daughter and by my son. As director of Baykeeper's Oyster Restoration Program, Meredith works to improve water quality and increase species richness in New York harbor; Nicholas has cared for animals, wild and tame. Both have reminded me of what is due the natural world, which is also ours. Lastly, I acknowledge, with profound feeling, my wife, Helen, whose unquestioning love for forty-seven years has been the mainstay and the saving of my life.

A further acknowledgment. Huck Finn said about Mark Twain, "He told the truth, mainly." Likewise, I've given myself license to do what storytellers must, in aid of a higher truth and a livelier yarn — that is, to play fast and loose, on occasion, with history — its places, persons, and incidents. Any historians among this novel's readers will, I hope, pardon my liberties.

Excerpts originally appeared in *Blue Earth Review* and *Green Mountains Review.*

ABOUT THE AUTHOR

Norman Lock's novel *The Boy in His Winter* (2014) and his story collection *Love Among the Particles* (2013) were also published by Bellevue Literary Press. Recently, his play *The House of Correction* was performed in Istanbul and Athens; his radio drama *Mounting Panic* was produced by WDR Germany. He has won *The Paris Review* Aga Khan Prize for Fiction and the Dactyl Foundation for the Arts & Humanities Literary Fiction Award, and writing fellowships from the New Jersey Council on the Arts (1999, 2013), the Pennsylvania Council on the Arts (2009), and the National Endowment for the Arts (2011). Norman lives in Aberdeen, New Jersey, nearby Raritan/Lower New York Bay, with his wife, Helen.

The employees of Thorndike Press hope you have enjoyed this Large Print book. All our Thorndike, Wheeler, and Kennebec Large Print titles are designed for easy reading, and all our books are made to last. Other Thorndike Press Large Print books are available at your library, through selected bookstores, or directly from us.

For information about titles, please call:

(800) 223-1244

or visit our Web site at:

http://gale.cengage.com/thorndike

To share your comments, please write:

Publisher
Thorndike Press
10 Water St., Suite 310
Waterville, ME 04901